# Logan's eyes turned electric

Paige felt shimmery shocks of electricity that skated along her nerve endings until she ached. All she wanted was to feel—one more time—what it was like to be held by Logan, kissed by Logan, loved by Logan.

The heat in his own eyes convinced her that Logan was feeling the same way. "Paige." His voice was so low and rough. "Tell me to go."

Her heartbeat was a crazy, mixed-up symphony inside her. She knew she should send him away, but her mouth wouldn't form the words.

He stepped forward until his body was only inches from hers. She could feel the heat coming off him.

Paige gasped as his lips brushed against her own. Her hands slid up his chest, vaguely cataloging the hard muscles there before she slipped them into the shaggy hair at the base of his neck and tried to tug him closer. If this moment was the only one she would have with him, she would grab it with both hands and say to hell with the consequences—at least for the duration of this one, perfect kiss.

Dear Reader,

I think the best romance is a combination of reality and fairy tale. A damsel or prince in distress, a damsel or prince to do the rescuing and a big, ugly dragon that needs slaying. In *Deserving of Luke,* I have all that and more, although the ugly dragon is not a tangible thing. Instead it is the very painful past the characters share, a past that they must slay together if they have any hope of finding their happily-ever-after.

Paige is a tough cookie who has been on her own—with her child—since she was seventeen years old. She's not only survived, but flourished, without much help. But she can't live that way forever, and watching as she learns to rely on Logan has been a wonderful journey—though it is one fraught with anger, perceived betrayal and hurt. It does have friendship, laughter and, eventually, love, though.

Logan, on the other hand, has pretty much had things easy. Seeing him learn to fight for what he wants—and for those who need him—was amazing. He has a long journey to finally be *Deserving of Luke,* his only son.

Speaking of Luke, I had so much fun creating his character. Some of my readers have noticed that when I create children they are almost all boys, and that is because, in this case, I really do write what I know. With three adorable and exasperating boys of my own to draw from, it's always easy for me to come up with a quip or an antic or a sweet little story that springs directly from my own life.

I really enjoyed writing *Deserving of Luke,* and hope you enjoy reading it, as well. Thank you so much for letting me—and my stories—into your hearts and lives. I love to hear from my readers via my website, www.tracywolff.com, or on my blog, www.tracywolff.blogspot.com. I wish each of you a wonderful, joy-filled spring!

Love,

Tracy Wolff

# Deserving of Luke
## *Tracy Wolff*

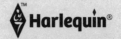

TORONTO NEW YORK LONDON
AMSTERDAM PARIS SYDNEY HAMBURG
STOCKHOLM ATHENS TOKYO MILAN MADRID
PRAGUE WARSAW BUDAPEST AUCKLAND

Recycling programs
for this product may
not exist in your area.

ISBN-13: 978-0-373-71703-3

DESERVING OF LUKE

Copyright © 2011 by Tracy L. Deebs-Elkenaney

## ABOUT THE AUTHOR

Tracy Wolff collects books, English degrees and lipsticks and has been known to forget where—and sometimes who—she is when immersed in a great novel. At six she wrote her first short story—something with a rainbow and a prince—and at seven she forayed into the wonderful world of girls' lit, reading her first Judy Blume novel. By ten she'd read everything in the young adult and classics sections of her local bookstore, so in desperation her mom started her on romance novels. And from the first page of the first book, Tracy knew she'd found her lifelong love. *Deserving of Luke,* her sixth novel for Harlequin Superromance, takes place on the gorgeous Oregon coast she loves to visit.

**Books by Tracy Wolff**

**HARLEQUIN SUPERROMANCE**

1529—A CHRISTMAS WEDDING
1568—FROM FRIEND TO FATHER
1607—THE CHRISTMAS PRESENT
1649—BEGINNING WITH THEIR BABY
1676—UNGUARDED

Don't miss any of our special offers. Write to us at the following address for information on our newest releases.

Harlequin Reader Service
U.S.: 3010 Walden Ave., P.O. Box 1325, Buffalo, NY 14269
Canadian: P.O. Box 609, Fort Erie, Ont. L2A 5X3

For my boys

## CHAPTER ONE

PANIC SET IN ABOUT FIVE minutes after Paige Matthews realized her son was gone.

At first, she told herself it was no big deal. He was probably two rows over in the toy aisle, checking to see if the selection was up to snuff.

When he wasn't there, poring over the surprisingly extensive collection of miniature cars, she figured he'd simply wandered over to the ice cream case—Luke was a sucker for strawberry ice cream.

And when he wasn't there either, when the small kernel of concern that had formed the moment she realized he was not at the end of the aisle as she'd thought he was, started to grow, she still told herself she was overreacting. This mom-and-pop grocery store in the small Oregon town she'd grown up in was a far cry from the huge supermarkets of Los Angeles, where Luke had been born and raised. Even at eight, he knew how to take care of himself, knew not to talk to strangers and to stay in one place if, for some reason, he did get separated from her—though it had never happened before.

So what could possibly happen to him here?

The reassuring thoughts didn't keep her from walking faster any more than they kept her from remembering her childhood here in Prospect and all the trouble she had managed to get into. While the fact that they weren't in the big city made her feel a little better, the feeling didn't last long—especially when she got to the candy aisle and realized Luke hadn't wandered over there, either. Worse, the store's display of gummy animals and body parts was completely undisturbed, a sure sign that he had not stopped here at all. And that was so unlike him that concern turned to terror.

"Luke!" she called, racing past the deserted candy section to the front of the store. "Luke, where are you?"

There was no answer and in those moments every terrible thing that *could* happen to an unaccompanied eight-year-old boy flashed through her mind, small town be damned. Sure, this was Prospect, but Eugene really wasn't that far away. Salem. Portland. All reasonably sized cities with rising crime rates.

"Luke!" She was running now, from one end of the store to the other, looking down each row that sprouted from the perimeter of the store.

Other shoppers stared at her, whispered, but she didn't acknowledge them. They'd whispered about her for the first seventeen years of her life—right up until she'd left town, broke and alone, save for the unborn baby she carried. The fact that they started talking about her so readily, even after all this time, came as no surprise. She might have been back for only a day and a half, but she knew how this town worked.

Some things never changed.

This time at least there was something real to talk about. Sure, she was running around like a crazy woman, but if they knew she was looking for her son, maybe someone else would start to look. Maybe someone else would spot him. Finding Luke, making sure he was safe, was the only thing that mattered.

But—surprise, surprise—no one came forward to help.

*Where could he be?* she wondered again as she frantically combed the aisles for her son's yellow and purple hoodie. She'd bought him the outrageously expensive jacket for his eighth birthday and he rarely went anywhere without it.

Why, oh, why, had she let Mary Beth Peters distract her? She didn't even like the woman—never had, even when they were in school together. Mary Beth had been the most popular girl in school and Paige had been…popular in her own right. But certainly not because she was head cheerleader.

Still, when Mary Beth had stopped her, Paige hadn't wanted to be rude. Hadn't wanted to cause

any more gossip than was absolutely necessary—
her sister Penny had to live and work here long after
Paige and Luke went home, after all. And she figured
alienating the locals was not the best way to reconcile
with her sister.

And look what her concern had gotten her. One
of these days she was going to remember that trying
to keep on the right side of these people's opinions
cost too much.

"Luke!" Paige screamed his name as adrenaline
coursed through her ice-cold body. She was ap-
proaching the last section of the grocery store and if
he wasn't there— If he wasn't there, she didn't know
how she was going to hold it together long enough to
call the sheriff's department.

She'd only spoken to Mary Beth for a couple of
minutes, long enough to exchange pleasantries and
a quick explanation about why she was back after
such a long time. How could her son have possibly disappeared in less than one hundred and eighty
seconds?

Suddenly she spotted the familiar L.A. Lakers
hoodie. "Luke." This time it wasn't a scream so much
as a long, exhale of relief. Grinding to a halt, she
rubbed her eyes to make sure she wasn't hallucinat-
ing. She wasn't. He was still there. Her son—her
beautiful, amazing, mischievous son—was seated
in front of the small comic-book display, the iPod

he'd gotten yesterday from his aunt Penny playing in his ears as he flipped through the latest superhero comic.

She blinked rapidly to clear her vision of the moisture that flooded her eyes—a shock in and of itself as it had been years since she'd allowed herself the luxury of anything as useless as tears. For so long it had been just Luke and her against the world. If anything ever happened to him she would—

Paige shook her head, unable to think about such a nightmarish occurrence, even in the abstract.

She didn't go to him right away, didn't wrap her arms around him and squeeze him the way she wanted to. Doing that before she had herself under control might trigger a public crying jag. A really bad idea here in the middle of Prospect hell.

Luke chose that moment to look up, and his not-quite-little-boy-anymore face lit up at the sight of her. "Hey, Mom! Look, it's the new one." He jumped nimbly to his feet, raced toward her. "Can I get it?"

Forcing herself not to grab him, Paige gently pulled one of the earbuds free. "You wander away from me in a public place and you expect me to reward you for it?" she asked in the sternest voice she could muster. It might have worked, too, except for the fact that her voice—like the rest of her—shook.

She saw the knowledge register in Luke's eyes, followed swiftly by a look of shame. "I'm sorry, Mom.

I went to find the gummy eyeballs and then found these instead. I didn't mean to scare you."

She tried to hang tough, but felt herself cave in the face of his obvious remorse. Taking the comic from Luke, she herded him to where she'd left her cart. She tossed the book on top of the fresh fruits and vegetables and told herself not to sweat it. She wasn't normally so lenient, but the joy of finding him clouded her judgment. She'd transplanted the kid from everything he knew to this small town next to nowhere. If a comic helped get him through the interminable summer, who was she to argue?

"Don't ever do it again. I couldn't find you and ran screaming through the store."

"Ugh, Mom, that so isn't the first impression I was hoping to make." Luke glanced toward a couple of boys who appeared close to his age. Both were staring at them as though they were alien life-forms. She didn't have the heart to tell Luke it was probably more about the nasty things they'd heard their mothers say about her than her mad dash through the store.

Prospect had a long memory, and no matter how much she'd accomplished in the nine years since she'd left here, she was still that wild Matthews girl from the wrong side of the river. The one whose mother had conceived her while her husband was serving his country overseas, then left her to wear the Scarlet A.

It was a legacy that had proved impossible to live down no matter how hard Paige tried, so in the end, she'd done her best to live up to it. It had been lonely, but infinitely more satisfying than crying herself to sleep every night had been.

At the moment, hearing the echoes of whispers and taunts and boys asking her for things she had been all too eager to give in her search for affection, she wished that she'd never come back. Never let Penny talk her into returning to this one-horse town, even if it was just for a few months.

But then, the wish was nothing new—she'd been repeating variations of it since she and Luke had rolled into town the day before. Before that actually, if she was completely honest with herself. That first pang of regret hit before she'd hung up the phone. Only the awareness that her sister was finally reaching out to her after so many years, that Penny needed her, had kept Paige's foot on the gas pedal and her car pointed north during the long trip.

"Come on, Luke, let's go." She hustled her son to the checkout. "You know you're not supposed to wander away like that. Anything could happen— especially in a place you don't know."

Luke stared at her in disbelief. "Mom, this place has a population of, like, five people. Nothing's going to happen to me here."

"More like five thousand people and you don't

know that nothing will happen to you. No one does."
God knew, plenty had happened to her in this sleepy
seaside town. More than enough that she had gotten
the hell out and never looked back. Until Penny's
desperate call for help—too embarrassed and afraid
to ask their parents for it.

That vulnerability, that fear, had been impossible
for Paige to ignore. She'd turned her back on Penny
once, had all but cut her sister from her life in her bid
for survival. She couldn't, wouldn't, do that again.
And if it cost her a little of her hard-won sanity, oh
well.

Something in her voice must have tipped Luke
off, because he stopped arguing much more quickly
than usual. "I'm really sorry, Mom."

"I know you are. Just, please, stay with me. You
don't know the town yet."

"I know. I promise I won't do it again." His silver
eyes shined with remorse.

"Good. Because next time I won't be so nice." She
was rubbing his back even as she made the threat,
leaning down to press a quick kiss on his rumpled
black curls and marveling—not for the first time—at
how incredibly blessed she was to have him. Prior
to Luke's arrival, her luck with men had been so
abysmal that when she'd found out she was having a
boy, she'd actually broken down and sobbed in the
ultrasound room.

But that was before she'd had him, before she'd held him. Before she'd known him. From the moment he'd entered the world, Luke had been the most amazing creature. Gorgeous, smart and with a heart full of joy and eyes full of mischief, he made every day an adventure. She wouldn't trade him for the world—and certainly not for a perfectly coiffed, well-behaved little girl. Any gray hair he gave her would be more than worth it. She was certain of it.

"Thanks for the comic, Mom. It's really cool."

Paige emptied her cart onto the conveyer belt as she listened to Luke rattle on about the adventures of his favorite superhero-bad-guy duo. She should have thought to check the book aisle for him first. Would have, had she known the store carried them. When she'd been a kid, the only books old Mr. Marshall had allowed into his store were religious and nature ones. Obviously, some things *had* changed in Prospect.

But not too many, she acknowledged wryly, hyperconscious of the not quite whispered comments currently circulating the market.

"Isn't that Paige Matthews? What's she doing here?"

"Always knew she was no good. Unwed mother—"

"Losing her child on her first day back—"

"Come to stay with her sister, in that pitiful little B and B—"

"She must be broke and is mooching off Penny—"

"I don't think she's broke. Did you see her car? Must be some drug dealer's girlfriend—"

Paige slammed her purse down on the small check-writing counter, and began bagging the groceries as the clerk—a teenaged girl who didn't seem to be aware of the barbed chatter—asked if she was new in town. Normally, bagging your own groceries was considered the height of rudeness in Prospect, as it indicated a desire to leave instead of participating in a nice, long chat. But being thought rude was the least of Paige's problems, so she shoved a head of broccoli into the same bag as a loaf of bread and a chocolate bar and prepared to call it a day.

"We're here for the summer," Luke told the girl with his quick, easy grin. "Mom says she's going to teach me to surf."

"Oh, yeah?" The girl looked impressed. "I've always wanted to learn how to do that myself."

"Well, maybe my mom can teach you, too. She's really good at it."

Paige laughed. "By *really good*, he means I fall off the board only about half the time." She put the last bag in the basket. "How much do I owe you?"

"Ninety-seven forty."

"And she's taking me for lunch at Prospector's," Luke continued. "She says they make the best strawberry shakes in all of Oregon."

"Maybe in the whole universe," the girl agreed.

"And they're even better if you have them throw a banana in with the strawberry ice cream."

"Really?" Luke looked skeptical.

"I swear."

He turned to Paige. "Can I try one, Mom? Please? I *looooove* bananas."

Cursing under her breath because she'd completely forgotten her promise to take her son for lunch, Paige forced a smile, even as she prayed for patience. "You can have whatever kind of shake you want as long as you eat some vegetables with lunch. Sound fair?"

Luke groaned, but agreed, "Sounds fair."

After signing the credit card slip and handing it to the girl, Paige let Luke push the basket to the car. Watching him carefully maneuver around the other vehicles made her smile, despite the worry that lingered in the corners of her mind. What was she going to do if Luke clued in to what kind of reputation his mother had had when she'd run away from this old-fashioned bastion of bigotry?

And how was she going to explain her reasons for doing what she'd done to him? He was already the only kid in his private-school class who didn't at least know who his dad was—something he seemed to be taking reasonably well. But she wasn't sure what old gossip could do to him—and she didn't want to find out.

One thing was for sure, she vowed as she slid into

the driver's seat. After today, she was going to do her damnedest to keep him away from this place and the people who wanted nothing more than to hurt him, simply because he was hers.

Whoever had said ignorance was bliss definitely knew what he was talking about.

## CHAPTER TWO

IT WAS A BEAUTIFUL DAY, the kind that made Logan Powell grateful he'd returned to Prospect after his big-city marriage had failed. Oh, he'd liked Seattle well enough—if you didn't mind the fact that it rained something like eighty-seven percent of the time. But after Melissa had left him he'd been ready for a change. And the fact that he'd been shot, had nearly bled to death in a drug bust gone bad, hadn't hurt his desire to return home, either. Prospect was the epitome of a sleepy coastal town and he liked it that way.

After parking his cruiser in the first available spot, Logan stepped into the street. He took a deep breath, held it in his lungs as long as he could before letting it out. In that breath was everything he loved about Prospect—sunshine, salt water and an abundance of greenery.

A glance at his watch told him he had plenty of time before he was supposed to meet his date at Prospector's, the local sixties diner, so he decided to take the long way around. There might not be much crime in Prospect, but that didn't mean he didn't take his job as sheriff seriously. These people depended on him and he wasn't going to let them down.

Today was a perfect time to weave his way through the tree-lined streets and check on the local businesses. It was a little early in the season for tourists to be descending, so he could enjoy this duty that would soon become a chore. He would still patrol the streets once they were packed with people in shorts and sundresses, haggling for antiques and beach shells, but the camaraderie he experienced now would be swallowed by strangers' demands.

Completely content with his lot in life, Logan took his time strolling the heavily shaded streets. The sun was shining, a nice breeze wound its way between the buildings and, in the background, the ocean crashed soothingly onto the sand. Yes, it really was a beautiful day.

As he made his way down Sycamore to Main, he whistled a little tune, something happy he remembered from his childhood. Perhaps he'd stop by the clinic to see if Jake was on call tonight. If he wasn't, maybe his old friend would be up for a few hands of poker. Logan was feeling lucky, and since the bastard had scalped him in their regular first Thursday of the month game, he owed him a chance to recoup his losses.

He'd barely stepped onto Main Street before

realizing the streets—and the people walking down them—were abuzz about something. Of course, it didn't take much to get the residents up in arms.

He wondered if Mr. Walker's Rottweiler had escaped again, plowing into God-only-knew whom. Or if the Harbinger brothers had gotten into another fight in the middle of Town Square. The last time it had happened they'd nearly killed themselves and he'd been stuck hauling both of them to jail. Before all was said and done he'd ended up with a black eye and his own assault case against the two of them. He'd let the charges drop on the understanding that they kept their differences non-violent in the future. But if they'd been fighting again—

"Morning, Sheriff." Marge Hutchinson's brusque voice pulled him from his reverie.

"Morning, Mrs. Hutchinson." He smiled at the boutique owner who had been slipping him a piece of red licorice behind his mother's back since he was three years old. "How are you this morning?"

"I'm doing just fine. Gearing up for the tourist rush."

"Glad to hear it. They should be here before you know it."

"Another week or two at the most. Bob's talked me into carrying some fancy soaps and perfumes. You should stop by and check them out," she said with a wink. "Maybe pick up something for your new girl."

He laughed. "Maybe I'll do that." Today's lunch was only his second date with Joni—the first had been a cup of coffee a few days ago—but already the town had the two of them paired up. It didn't annoy him the way it did some. Instead, it amused him. Where else but Prospect would his love life be a public service project?

"Good. I'll set some of the gardenia products aside. They'll smell real good on Joni. And you'll be needing them after she finds out—" She looked away, her crimson painted lips pressed tightly together.

His radar went on red alert. "After she finds out what, Mrs. Hutchinson?"

"I suppose I should just tell you. It's better than you hearing it from one of those old busybodies down the street."

He barely bit back a smile. She was one of the busiest bodies in town. Despite her feigned reluctance, she was probably rejoicing in the fact that she'd beaten Ruth Oberly to the punch.

"Well, I was in the grocery store earlier today and you'll never guess who's back in town."

She glanced at him, as if waiting for him to guess despite her words, but he didn't have a clue. He rarely kept track of the tourists who came and went, even the ones who returned year after year.

Leaning forward, as if she had a particularly juicy secret to impart, Mrs. Hutchinson took her time drawing out the suspense. "I might not have even noticed her, except for the fact that she'd lost her son. *Lost her son,* can you believe it? On her first day back in town."

He felt a premonition that he wasn't going to like whatever came out of her mouth next. "Did they find the boy?" he demanded. "The sheriff's department hasn't been notified—"

"Oh, yes, they found him after only a couple of minutes, hiding in the back with the comic books. But not before she made a total spectacle of herself running around screaming for him." She sniffed. "He didn't answer. Not that I blame him, I guess. If I had her for a mother, I'd probably be hiding, too. It probably looked like a good place to stay lost, as not many people make it back there."

Patience wearing thin after her salacious account— it wasn't like Mrs. Hutchinson to be so malicious and it made him uncomfortable to be a part of it, even if in a peripheral way—Logan asked, "So who is it? Who's back in town?"

She grinned. "Paige Matthews. And from the amount of food she picked up at the grocery store, she's planning on staying a while."

Her words sent him reeling, the way she'd intended them to. She kept talking, telling him more—he was sure—about Paige's ill-fated trip to the market, but he didn't hear her. *Couldn't* hear her over the buzzing in his ears and the shock that was ricocheting through him.

Paige Matthews was back in town.

Paige was back.

In town.

*Paige Matthews was back in town.*

The words looped in his mind as he tried to figure out what they meant when strung together in that order.

Trying to get them to make sense.

And more than anything, trying to decide how he felt about them.

Fumbling an excuse he knew didn't make much sense, he headed up the street in a kind of daze. He knew Mrs. Hutchinson—and plenty of other people— were watching him, but in those first few moments, he couldn't bring himself to care. Couldn't bring himself to fake his way through this bombshell.

It had been so long since he'd heard anything about Paige, so long since he'd even allowed himself to think her name.

He didn't get far before someone else stopped him to report the same news. Again and again, people stepped forward to tell him about Paige, each one adding a new little detail about her—and her son— until he felt as though he'd run the gauntlet.

Had he seen what kind of car she was driving? one person asked.

A ninety-thousand-dollar BMW, someone else imparted. Of course, she'd gotten it illegally. Hadn't they always known she was going to turn out to be a drug dealer's girlfriend? He'd tried to put that rumor to rest by mentioning the latest movie she'd been involved with, but he'd known his protests had fallen on deaf ears when the same person asked if he thought Paige was on the run from her drug-dealing boyfriend.

Did he know why she was back?

Logan's simple morning walk through town had turned into a nightmare. And for the life of him, he couldn't figure out why he cared.

Yes, he and Paige had been an item a million years ago. And, yeah, she'd screwed him over totally and completely. But that didn't mean he wished her ill, didn't mean he wanted any of the things the townspeople were speculating about to be true. Any more than it meant he wanted to see her.

Sure, he might be curious about what she'd been up to. And why she had chosen now—when he'd been in Prospect a little over eighteen months and was finally getting comfortable with his new life—to come back to town. But it didn't matter. It wasn't like he would be asking her any of those questions any time soon.

If they met up, *when* they met up—this was Prospect after all, and there were only so many places to frequent—he would be polite, courteous. Treat her the way he did any of the other people under his protection. Because that's what she was to him—all she would ever be to him. Maybe she'd meant something to him in the past, but that was a long time ago. The present and future were a whole different story.

He was the first to admit he'd made a lot of mistakes in his life. But from the time he was a kid, he'd made a point of not making the same mistake twice.

And Paige had been more than a youthful mistake. She'd been a goddamned natural disaster that had ripped apart the very fabric of his life. And it had taken him too long to get over her to ever let her back in again.

Pasting a wide—and hopefully not glazed—smile on his lips, Logan continued toward the diner in as straight a line as he could manage. He didn't know much about Paige anymore, but he knew he was going to lose it if he had to hear one more ridiculous rumor about her. Or her son.

Then Ruth Oberly stepped into his path and asked if he'd had a chance to see Paige Matthews's son yet. When he'd told her he hadn't, she'd looked at him blandly and said that she thought the boy looked just like his father.

Logan's back went ramrod straight at this new piece of information, and he had to force himself to relax. Normally, he didn't mind the gossip that was part and parcel of living in a small town—it was relatively harmless, after all—but Paige's child was still a raw spot for him.

The knowledge came as a surprise, and not a pleasant one. In fact, he was so busy trying to wrap his mind around the implication that one look at the kid had given Ruth a good idea of who his father was, that he nearly missed the diner. Logan had spent a lot of hours trying to convince Paige to tell him the truth about which of his high-school classmates had gotten her pregnant and the thought that he might finally be able to find out, after all these years, had him reeling.

Which was perfectly normal, he assured himself. It wasn't as if they didn't have history together. After Paige had left Prospect, he'd spent weeks—months— lying awake wondering about her. Wondering if she was okay. Wondering if the father of her kid was helping her out. Every time one of the guys from Paige's side of the river had left town, Logan had wondered if he was the one. If he was sneaking off to be with Paige, wherever she was.

Eventually he'd left himself, gone to college, and memories of her had faded to bittersweet regret. Sure, she'd creep up on him sometimes, but he figured that was normal, when all was said and done.

First love was a bitch, after all. Sure, he'd gotten over her, moved on with his life, even gotten married to a woman he'd loved. But that didn't mean memories of Paige—memories of them—didn't catch him off guard every once in a while. They'd sneak in when he least expected it—a glimpse of the swings at the park, the teasing scent of lilac in the woods, a stray word about her sister and the crazy house Penny had bought with the hope of turning it into a bed and breakfast—and suddenly he'd be right back there, crazy in love with a girl his parents wouldn't let in the front door.

But that's all they were, he assured himself. Just memories. And if hearing about her son was a kick in the ass, the sting would quickly fade. After all, her betrayal had happened a long time and a lot of women ago. He had more important things to worry about these days than ancient history.

And yet, he found himself thinking about her. The idea that Paige was here now, that the answers to all those old questions were suddenly within his reach, had him thinking about things that were better laid to rest.

Frustrated, out-of-sorts, his earlier enjoyment of the day completely gone, Logan pushed open the door to the diner. And got a hell of a start when nearly every face turned toward him, the low buzz of conversation coming to an abrupt halt.

Okay. Never comfortable being the obvious topic of conversation he reminded himself of all the positive reasons to living in a town where he knew well over half the population. There was always someone to talk to, always someone around to lend a hand.

Even with the good points outweighing the bad, it didn't mean it was always easy. Especially not when people were interested to see what his reaction would be to the knowledge that Paige, and her son, were back in town. Well, they'd learn soon enough it was no big deal. He and Paige were nothing to each other anymore.

Glancing around the diner with a friendly smile, he breathed a small sigh of relief when his gaze landed on Joni. There was nothing like a date with one woman to lay old gossip about another to rest.

Grinning for real this time, he started toward her table. There was nothing wrong with him, a hamburger, a piece of peach pie and some time with Joni wouldn't fix.

Focused on his target, Logan didn't see Paige until he was almost on top of her. And when it finally registered on him that the pretty woman at the next table was the grown-up version of his high-school sweetheart, it was too late to do anything but stare.

And stare he did, his mind cataloguing all the

differences between this woman and the girl he remembered. Her platinum-blond hair was a lot shorter,
cut into a sassy style that suited the woman, but not
the vulnerable young girl who'd once confided to him
that she liked him because she didn't have to play a
part for him.

Her heart-shaped face was thinner, her cheekbones
more prominent, her green eyes darker and more
wary than they had ever been. Only her lips were
the same—lush and a little lopsided, their raspberry
color as tempting as ever.

She was wearing a violet tank top that showed off
curves much more lush than he remembered and,
though he told himself to move on, to pull out a chair
at Joni's table, he didn't move. Instead, he stood there,
willing Paige to look at him.

At first, he didn't think she was going to, thought
she was going to pretend to be oblivious to his presence. But as he contemplated doing something stupid
to get her attention, she met his gaze with her own
unflinching stare. For one long, indefinable second,
it was as if they were back in high school, when it
had been only the two of them no matter how many
other people were in the room.

He heard her catch her breath, felt his own hitch
in his chest. His hand reached out to her of its own
volition and it took every ounce of self-control he
had not to trace the familiar dusting of freckles on

her cheeks, as if nine years and countless arguments didn't lay between them.

He started to say something, stopped. Tried again, stopped again. Then the moment was gone, her attention diverted by a young voice asking, "Mom, can I get my milkshake now? I ate all my green beans."

Her expression appeared stricken before she turned her attention to her son. For a second Logan couldn't figure out what was wrong. Then he looked toward the boy sitting across from her, his black curls gleaming under the restaurant's warm, yellow lights, and Logan's entire world caved in.

He felt his jaw slacken and his eyes widen as a thousand different questions exploded in his head. As he looked over Paige's son, Logan told himself that it couldn't be. That he had to be mistaken. That Paige wouldn't have his child without telling him.

The words circled his brain, a particularly ineffectual mantra. Because even as he was talking to himself, even as he was trying to convince himself that he was wrong, that he was making a huge mistake, he knew he wasn't. This child—this lively, *eight-year-old* boy with the silver eyes and small birthmark on his right cheek—was his *son* and he didn't even know the kid's name.

The realization was a blow that nearly brought him to his knees. Shock and sorrow warred within him, followed by the beginnings of a rage so powerful it made him shake.

His child had existed in the world for eight years and he hadn't known.

His child had grown and laughed, hurt and played, for eight years and he hadn't known.

His child had—

"Hello, Logan."

Screw pleasantries. There was only one thing he wanted from her. "Why didn't you tell me?"

Paige raised one blond eyebrow, smiled serenely, coolly as if the same moments that had just blown Logan's world to hell and back had barely affected her.

"I did tell you. You chose not to believe me."

That was it. No explanation, no plea for forgiveness, no acknowledgment of guilt. A few simple words that did nothing to lower his blood pressure, and nothing to set this situation to rights.

"You know that's a bunch of bull—"

"No milkshake today," she announced to her son, to *their son*.

As much as Logan resented her interruption, the still-functioning part of his brain appreciated it. This was not the place—in full view of the curious patrons, of his date…of their son—to give vent to the rage boiling inside him.

"We'll get one next time," she continued, speaking

to their boy. "We need to get back soon or Aunt Penny's going to send the cavalry after us."

The boy rolled his eyes. "There's no cavalry anymore, Mom. Now the army uses tanks." He turned to Logan. "Who are you?"

Logan had no idea where to begin to answer that, so he kept quiet. Let Paige field the question.

"He's just someone I used to know. Back when I was in high school." She reached for her purse. "And the fact that there's no cavalry anymore is an even better reason for us to head home. Can you imagine a tank rolling down Main Street?"

"That'd be cool! Do you think it would point its big gun at the diner?"

"I can only hope." With that cryptic comment, Paige stood, dropped some money on the table then herded her child toward the door.

Damn it, the child was *his*. Not only hers, *his*, too. And he had no clue what to call him. "What's his name?" Logan demanded, loud enough for the whole restaurant to hear. Not that he cared. Worrying about what others thought seemed worse than stupid when he was watching his child walking away from him without a backward glance.

She turned then, and it was the first hint he had she might be experiencing the same anger he was. "None of your damn business."

Then she was gone, leaving behind a silence so complete that the slamming of the door echoed like a gunshot.

PAIGE COULD BARELY CONTROL the fury as she headed toward her car.

How dare Logan try to embarrass her in public?

How dare he accuse her of not telling him about Luke when she had *begged* him to believe that she was carrying his child?

How *dare* he pick this fight in front of Luke?

If she had ever needed more proof of what an abysmal father he would make, she'd gotten it. He hadn't cared about Luke's feelings, hadn't cared about anything but his own righteous outrage. Bastard. The next time he came around—if there was a next time—she would run him off with a baseball bat if she had to, small-town cop or not. No way was that son of a bitch getting anywhere near her son. Not now. Not after all this time. She'd see him in hell first.

"Mom, slow down!"

She'd been so locked in her thoughts she hadn't noticed Luke scrambling along beside her, his short legs working overtime in an effort to keep up.

"I'm sorry, sweetie." She stopped abruptly, tapped Luke on the nose. "I forget sometimes that your legs aren't as long as mine."

"Why are you so mad? Is it because of that guy?" he asked as they resumed walking, though at a much more sedate rate.

"I'm not angry. I just didn't realize how late it had gotten. The delivery men are going to be at Aunt Penny's any minute and I need to be there to tell them where to put the supplies. If I'm not, she'll end up letting them put the stuff anywhere and it will be a disaster." She paused, ruffled his hair. "Unless you want to help me haul everything upstairs to all the bedrooms?"

"Yeah, right. You nearly killed me the last time we did that."

"Exactly."

They lapsed into silence, but Paige didn't delude herself into thinking that Luke was going to buy her answer about Logan for long.

Sure enough, as she hit the button to unlock the car doors Luke ambushed her. "Was that man my dad?"

She stared at him, mouth open, as her brain scrambled for an answer. She didn't want to lie to him, knew if she did it would turn around and bite her in the ass. After all, eventually she'd have to admit to Luke that, yes, Logan was his father.

But how could she do that now? How could she blurt it out in the middle of the street as though it was no big deal? Luke might be advanced for his age,

but he was still an eight-year-old boy. How much of
what had happened between her and Logan could
she expect him to understand?

She closed her eyes, prayed for divine intervention. Nothing. Seemed that truth was her only option.
"Yes. That was the man who fathered you."

Luke nodded, as though he'd been certain of it all
along. Knowing him, he probably had been. "Why
did he say you never told him about me?"

*Because he's a lying, deceitful, distrustful bas-
tard who wouldn't know the truth if it hit him over
the head*. The words were on the tip of her tongue
and she had to make a conscious effort to bite them
back. Jeez, and she'd thought she was over Logan's
betrayal? Obviously, denial wasn't only a river in
Egypt. It was alive and well in Prospect, Oregon, as
well.

She tilted his chin up so that Luke was looking
directly into her eyes. She didn't want there to be a
mistake about this, didn't want him to think for one
second that she resented him because of his father's
attitude toward her.

"I'm not sure why he said that. I suppose because
things between us weren't particularly good when we
broke up and he didn't want to believe that you were
his."

"Why not?"

*Because he's a lying, deceitful, distrustful bastard*

*who...* "I don't know, sweetie. I spent a lot of nights staring at the ceiling trying to answer that same question myself. But you know what?"

"It doesn't matter."

"What?"

"That's what you were going to say. 'It doesn't matter.' And you're right. It doesn't. We've done great without him so far, so who cares whether he wanted me or not?" He gave her a small smile right before he slipped into the car and closed the door gently behind him.

That action more than anything—more than the too quietly spoken, the too mature words, more than the pain in the smile—convinced her that her son missed having a father far more than she had ever known. Luke, so exuberant and full of life, only closed doors softly when he was badly hurt. Normally she had to remind him at least four or five times a day not to slam the door so hard.

They'd talked about his father through the years—of course they had. She didn't normally bring him up, but whenever Luke had asked about Logan she'd tried to be as honest as she could, without airing all of the difficulties and arguments they'd had after she had found out she was pregnant.

It had seemed to be enough for Luke, the knowledge that she loved him more than anything or anyone else on earth. She'd done everything in her power to make up for the fact that he didn't have a father, and she'd always thought she'd done a pretty good job of it. Luke hadn't even known he was missing a dad until he'd gone to kindergarten and figured out that almost all of his classmates had two parents, even if not all of them lived together.

They'd talked about it then, and numerous times since, but obviously she'd missed something. Sometime between kindergarten and third grade he'd decided she wasn't enough.

The knowledge hurt, even as she told herself she was being ridiculous. He was a boy—of course he'd missed having a father around. She'd expected that.

What she hadn't expected was for Luke to try to keep his feelings from her, to try to protect her from his pain when it was *her* job to protect *him*.

So how was she going to fix things? She walked around to her side of the car. How was she going to make things better for Luke when he was saddled with such a no-good jerk for a dad?

Part of her wanted to blame the town, wanted to blame Penny and her stupid bed-and-breakfast, for dragging them back here. They'd been doing okay in L.A. Better than okay. They'd been doing great. They had their groove, their routine, and it had worked for them.

Coming here had disrupted all that. It had hit her hard and had obviously had the same kind of effect on Luke, though he hadn't told her about it. But it had been stupid to think that it would all work out. That her smart, precocious child wouldn't figure out that in returning to her hometown, she was putting him—for the first time in his life—in close proximity to the man who had fathered him.

What had she thought? That if Logan saw them on the street he wouldn't make the connection? Or that if he did, he wouldn't care? After all, he hadn't tried to contact her once after she'd left town, hadn't so much as asked Penny where she'd gone. She knew that, because she'd asked her sister about him every time they'd spoken. Penny's answer had always been the same—Logan acted as if she didn't exist.

He'd cut her—and their child—out of his life so completely nine years ago that it was hard to imagine that he would suddenly have questions about that child. About *her* child.

Obviously, she'd been an idiot. Sighing, she opened the car door. It wasn't the first time she'd been stupid and it wouldn't be the last. But she was horribly sorry that her son had been caught in the middle of the whole, dirty affair.

She was about to slide into the car when Logan caught up to her.

"You think you can walk away from me like that?" he demanded, his voice low and furious. Despite herself, the tone sent shivers down her spine as it reminded her of all the fights they'd had when they'd been together. And all the making up they'd done when they'd gotten over the anger. "We haven't settled anything yet."

It was almost a whisper and her stomach tightened in response. Logan was one of the few people she knew whose voice actually got quieter the angrier he got. If he was yelling or cursing, it was no big deal. But the second his voice became deadly calm, she'd know she was in for it.

The day he'd kicked her out of his life, she'd had to strain to hear him.

This time she wasn't a stupid seventeen-year-old girl who worshipped the town's golden boy. This time she was a grown woman who was more than capable of holding her own against him, or anyone. She glanced into the car, caught a glimpse of Luke's rapt face, and knew that even though she could, she still wasn't going to take Logan on. Not here and not now, where her son could piece together how angry she was at his father.

"What I think is that now is not the time to deal with this. Luke is watching and the last thing he needs is to see the two of us fighting."

"What he needs is—"

Paige could tell it was taking every ounce of will-power Logan had not to continue with what he was saying. But he bit it back, bit back all the accusations

she could tell he wanted to level at her. She could see
them in the darkest depths of his silver eyes, see them
in his tense jaw and shoulders, in his fists.

Slowly, very slowly, his hands and jaw relaxed.
Then he blew out a long breath and said, "We need
to talk."

She wanted to disagree on general principle, to tell
him that there was nothing she wanted to talk to him
about. But another look at her son changed her mind.
Luke's fascination with Logan was hard to miss.

Swallowing the bitterness that welled inside of
her, she answered. "Yeah. I guess we do."

"When?"

"I don't know. In a few days—"

"A few days isn't acceptable. I want to talk to you
today."

"Yeah, well, I gave up worrying about what you
wanted a long time ago, Logan. I'm not here to see
you. I'm here to help my sister. So if you want to
talk to me, you're going to have to work around *my*
schedule."

"Your schedule? You have my kid and you have
the nerve to talk to me about schedules?"

A million responses came to her—none of which
were fit for polite company but all of which she
wanted to say. "How about tomorrow afternoon?"

"I want to talk to you today." He ground out the

words in a voice so harsh it hurt her ears. And still she wouldn't back down, wouldn't give in.

Her son was too important for her to roll over and play dead. And if his father thought differently, then he was in for a rude awakening. She'd never been one for power struggles, but on this front, she was digging in. There was no way he was going to move her.

"I want a lot of things. I always have. But part of growing up is realizing that you can't always have what you want. Isn't that what our mothers always used to tell us?"

For a second she thought Logan was going to lose the stranglehold he had on control and she regretted taunting him. Not because she was afraid of him—the Logan she knew would never hurt her physically and she'd kick his ass if he tried—but because Luke was watching. He didn't know what they were saying, which probably only made the tension between them look scarier.

Sure enough, his door cracked open a little. "Mommy. Are you okay?"

He never called her *Mommy* anymore, and she saw the second his words registered on Logan, the second the sheriff realized his son was afraid of what he would do to his mother. She watched as he forcibly made himself relax.

"I'm fine, sweetie. I'll be ready to go in a second."

"What time tomorrow afternoon?" Logan demanded.

She knew it cost him a lot to ask her that, to give in without a fight simply because it would be easier for Luke. And she gave Logan credit for it, though it was hard. She'd spent so long loving him and wishing he'd call, so long hating him because he hadn't, that it was almost impossible to give him even the slightest benefit of the doubt now. Especially when he was still as arrogant and gorgeous and out of line as he'd always been.

But she would. For her son's sake, she would give Logan a chance and pray to God that she wasn't making a mistake. "Why don't you come by Penny's house tonight, after ten? Luke usually goes to sleep around nine-thirty. We can talk then."

He nodded. "I'll see you at ten."

"Okay."

There was nothing left to say, and yet neither one of them made a move to leave. Instead they stood there looking at each other, the past yawning like a chasm between them, until Luke's door opened one more time.

"Mom?"

"I'm coming, Luke. We're done here."

Logan nodded, and left without another word. As

she watched him walk away, Paige prayed again that she wasn't making the biggest mistake of her life. That she wasn't making the biggest mistake of Luke's life.

# CHAPTER THREE

"How was town?" Penny asked as Luke and Paige lugged their grocery bags into the house almost an hour later.

"Pretty damn awful." Paige blew a stray hair out of her face. "I swear, I don't know how you can stand to live here. Nothing changes."

"That's not necessarily a bad thing, you know." Penny relieved her of a few of the bags.

"Easy for you to say. They don't look at you like you should come with a warning label—and a decontamination chamber—attached. I don't understand why you want to—" She broke off, refusing to ruin her time with Penny by bringing up an argument that dated to when they were kids. If they were going to fix everything that needed fixing—Penny's seaside house, her self-esteem after her boyfriend dumped her with this monstrosity, their sibling relationship, which hadn't been the same since Paige had left town nine years before—she needed to tread carefully.

"I stay here because this is home to me. I like it here," Penny blithely answered the unfinished question. "I know Prospect wasn't good for you, know you've done amazing things since you left. But this is the only place I've ever wanted to live. When I moved away, I missed it."

Paige's nod was stilted, but she was saved from responding when Luke found the treasure he'd been searching through the bags for. "Look, Aunt Penny. Mom bought me a totally cool comic book. Do you want to see it?"

"Of course I do. Maybe you could read it to me while I put these groceries away." She reached into a bag and pulled out a jar of pickles.

"And we ran into my dad in town. He was dressed in a policeman's uniform and he seemed really mad at Mom."

The jar of pickles slipped from her sister's hand and shattered as it hit the kitchen's hardwood floor.

"Why don't you sit down?" Paige said, tongue firmly in cheek. "I'll put the groceries away."

"You saw Logan and that's all you have to say?"

Shooting a warning look from her sister to her son, Paige nodded. "It's not quite as eloquent as dropping a jar of pickles, I know, but I do what I can."

"Right. Of course." Penny sounded as though she was being strangled, but she didn't say anything else as she started cleaning up the mess.

"Do you know my dad, Aunt Penny?"

She succumbed to a major coughing fit. When she

finally recovered, she said, "Um, I guess. A little bit. Why?"

"Because I don't think I like him. He was mean to Mom. On the way home, she said it was because he was surprised to see me, but I don't know. So I thought, if you knew him, you could tell me if you thought he was as bad as he seemed today." Luke said the last words in a rush, his breath running out from trying to say everything in one fell swoop. She could see the hope shining in his eyes, along with the fear and prayed that Penny could as well.

Tenderness for her son welled up inside Paige all over again, even as she felt torn apart by the fact that she was going to have to see Logan in a few hours. Luke was so sweet and he wanted this so badly, that she wanted to want it, too. But she couldn't. She just couldn't—not when giving him his father meant allowing Logan in her life again.

He'd done so much damage the first time around it had taken her years to stop reeling.

"I don't think your dad is awful, Luke," Penny finally said after an awkward silence. "I'm sure he wasn't trying to be mean to your mom. He was probably shocked to see you. He didn't know you were coming."

"He says he didn't know about me at all."

Penny's eyes darkened to forest green. "Well, then, he must have been confused."

"That's what Mom says."

"You should listen to your mother. She knows a lot more than your father does."

"Penny!" Paige frowned at her sister.

"Well, you do. Men are—"

"I don't really think Luke is up for a diatribe against the male species at the moment, sis, but thanks all the same."

"And yet I'm so clearly in the mood to have one." But she turned to Luke and forced a smile onto her face. And if more teeth showed than Paige was comfortable with, she figured she couldn't really complain. Especially not when Penny changed the subject by asking, "What else happened in town today?"

"Nothing much."

Luke became studiously interested in his comic book and Paige snorted. "If by *nothing much* you mean I ran through Mandala's Groceries like a crazy woman, than no, nothing much happened, Penny."

"Ran through Mandala's? What happened?"

Paige told her, and though she gave Luke a number of stern looks as she did, she couldn't help grinning when he interrupted several times to give Penny his point of view.

As he talked, Paige shook her head repeatedly—though she didn't know if it was with pride or annoyance. Or both. The kid had a future as a politician or an advertising exec. His gift of spin was truly awe-inspiring.

When the two of them had finished telling the story, Penny gave her nephew an admonishing look. "I think you owe your mom a week's worth of chores without complaint."

"But—"

Penny raised one dark eyebrow and Luke subsided. They hadn't been here long enough for him to get used to Penny yet. And with his new iPod burning a hole in his pocket, he jumped every time she told him to. A habit that was not lost on his aunt.

"In fact," she said, with a wink towards Paige, "why don't you start by going upstairs and finishing unpacking all of your toys? I hauled a bookshelf in there earlier, so you can spread them out. And I even dug up a TV, so you can move your Wii up there instead of down here."

"Excellent!" Luke nearly flew out of the room on his way upstairs. "I just got this cool new baseball game I want to try out."

"Luke! Aren't you forgetting—"

"Thanks, Aunt Penny." His voice drifted down the stairs.

Penny laughed. "I don't know how you keep up with that kid. He's a natural born charmer."

"Tell me about it. He's had every single one of his teachers wrapped around his little finger from the get-go, not to mention all the neighbors. They're convinced the sun rises and sets on his shoulders."

"Must make it hard to discipline him."

"You have no idea. No matter how in the right I am, I always end up looking like the bad guy. It drives me nuts."

"It always did."

Paige shot her a sharp look. "What's that supposed to mean?"

"It means, he's like his father, Paige. Everything about him—from his looks to the sparkle in his eyes—screams Logan. No wonder the man had a fit when he saw him today."

Paige didn't answer until she heard the door to the room she and Luke were sharing firmly shut. Then she turned on her sister. "He doesn't have any reason to throw a fit. He's the one who dumped me when I told him I was pregnant. He's the one who accused me of sleeping with half the football team. I told him Luke was his and he didn't believe me."

"A point I think you should bring up to him when you see him again." Penny paused. "I assume you will be seeing him again?"

"He's coming here later tonight, after Luke is in bed."

Her sister cursed. "That was quick."

"Tell me about it. I really thought I'd have a little more time before I had to deal with this."

"Me, too." She paused. "So what are you going to say to him?"

"That he hasn't been around for the first eight years of Luke's life and there's no reason he needs to be around for the next ten years of it. Luke and I are doing fine without him."

"Yeah? And do you think he's going to buy that?"

"Of course he's going to buy it. He couldn't wait to be rid of the responsibility when I was pregnant." Her voice cracked on the last word so Paige focused on emptying the bags in an effort to keep herself from freaking out. "No, Penny, I don't think he's going to be reasonable about this. You should have seen him in the diner. I thought he was going to blow a gasket."

"Is that where you guys met up? At Prospector's?"

"Naturally. Hasn't my dirty laundry always been aired in front of half the town?" She proceeded to tell Penny the whole sordid story. Her sister didn't say anything through most of it, just made sympathetic noises.

When she was done, Penny crossed the kitchen and pulled her into a huge hug. "I'm sorry you've got to deal with this guy again, Paige. He's a total jerk."

"Tell me about it. Nothing like paying for the mistakes of your youth forever, huh?"

"Yeah, well, you don't have to be young to be stupid," Penny said with a grimace.

Paige knew better than to express sympathy for Penny's current male-induced crisis—that was the quickest way to get her to shut down.

With a sigh, Paige rested her head on her sister's shoulder and said, "What am I going to do?"

"Whatever you want to do."

"I wish. If that was the case, I wouldn't let Logan near my kid."

"Then don't. You don't have to explain anything to that man. What he did to you is unforgivable and you don't owe him a damn thing."

"I know that."

"Do you?"

"Of course I do. But it's not him I'm worried about. It's Luke. And I do owe him the chance to get to know his father, if that's what he wants."

"He's eight. He doesn't know what he wants. If he knew Logan the way we do, he wouldn't be so quick to imagine how great his life would be with him."

"It's not that simple. Now that Logan knows about him, what am I supposed to do if he decides he wants to see Luke?"

"Tell him to buzz off. He had his chance nine years ago and if he suddenly decides that he regrets the choices he made, well, that's tough for him. Some mistakes can't be undone."

Paige nodded her agreement, but as she put the milk and eggs into the fridge, she couldn't help wondering if thinking that was unrealistic. Sure, she didn't think that Logan had any claim to Luke. They'd broken up nine years ago, with Logan telling her he wanted nothing to do with her or her baby. Why should he get to change his mind at this late date?

But as the sounds of Luke's video game console buzzed overhead, she felt a niggle of doubt. The Logan she'd known had been a cold bastard when it came to getting what he wanted—even at eighteen— but the man she'd met today had seemed downright frigid. If he wanted a part in Luke's life, she wasn't sure how she was going to stop him. Especially if he filed for custody here, in this town where everyone hated her. What if he actually succeeded in convincing a judge to take Luke away from her? She'd die. She would just—

Paige slammed a door on her thoughts, refusing to let them freak her out any more than she already was. If there was one thing her twenty-six years had taught her, it was that life would happen the way it was going to happen, no matter how much she worried about it. Besides, she had a lot better things to think about than the arrogant, devious ways of Logan Powell.

Even if she couldn't remember what any of those things were right now.

"He can't hurt you, you know," Penny said. "You won't let him. *I* won't let him. Not ever again."

Warmth filled Paige. "You know, for a bratty little sister, you're pretty awesome."

"For an obnoxious, know-it-all older sister you're not so bad yourself." Penny paused, and Paige desperately hoped for a shift in the conversation. But Penny didn't give it to her. "But seriously, Paige, how are we going to handle this?"

"*We?* It's my problem, Penny."

"The only reason you came back here is because I totally screwed my life up. I'd say that makes it *our* problem." She gestured to the paint cans and building supplies that filled up the living room. "I don't know how I'd get this place together without your help."

And there it was, the reason Paige had returned to Prospect even though it was the last place on the planet she wanted to be. She'd skipped out of town nine years ago, pregnant and devastated. But she'd left Penny alone with their parents, and though her mom and dad treated her sister a lot better than they'd ever treated her, it still hadn't been a cakewalk.

But Paige hadn't cared, hadn't let herself care. She couldn't if she wanted to survive. So she'd cut ties with her sister completely. And though Penny had reached out to her a year ago, trying to reestablish those ties, it had been slow going. At least until her fiancé had run away from her and this monstrosity of a house, leaving Penny almost broke and in a hell of a bind.

There had been no way Paige could leave her to muddle through on her own. Not when she was between set decorating jobs. She'd built in two weeks between movies to use as a vacation, but helping her sister was going to be so much more satisfying. And if she'd had to juggle things around and work like mad in order to make that two-week break a two-month break, well, then no one else had to know that.

"Luckily, you won't have to find out."

"But—and don't take this the wrong way as you know I love that you're here—but maybe you should go back to L.A. Get Luke away from Logan as fast as possible."

The same idea had occurred to her, oh, about every fifteen seconds since Logan had chased her down the street. "I'm afraid he'd follow me. He seems really determined to see Luke."

Penny snorted. "Yeah, nine years too late. But even if he follows you, won't that give you home court advantage. Literally? He's the sheriff here and one of the town's golden boys. Wouldn't it be better to fight this battle in a Los Angeles court?"

"I'm hoping it won't come to that."

"But if it does?"

"If it does, then yes. L.A. would probably be a better venue for it."

"Then don't feel the need to stick around here."

"Penny—"

"No, I mean it. If it's best for you and Luke, I want you to go back to California. As soon as possible."

The thought had appeal. Definite appeal. And yet— "I don't know if that's going to work. It might already be too late."

"How can it be too late? You just saw the man an hour ago."

Penny was right, Paige knew she was. But the doubts at the base of her spine told her she was already in too deep. That if she ran now, it would destroy any chance she had of dealing with Logan in a mature, low-key manner. "It just is. Trust me." She reached for a box of cereal. "Where do you want me to put this?"

"In my hand." Penny all but ripped it away from her and shooed her toward the back door. "Why don't you get out of here? You've had a rough day. I insist you relax for a few minutes while I finish putting this stuff away."

"I don't want to go relax. I'm so wound up that I might be able to orbit the planet under my own power."

"All the more reason to get out of here. A walk

on the beach will help you clear your head. Then we can make dinner together, before I challenge you to a virtual tennis match."

This time Paige's laugh *was* real. "We've been here less than two days and you're already as addicted to that Wii as Luke is."

"That's because it's all kinds of awesome. Now go."

Paige headed out the door, but stopped on the threshold. "You know, Mike was a fool."

"You won't get an argument from me. Waiting until I sank all my money into this place to make our dream come true before taking off. He deserves whatever bad karma he gets—and I hope it's a boatload. But I refuse to spend any more time being miserable over his disappearance. Not when it brought you back to me."

Unsure of how to deal with the naked emotion in her sister's eyes—honest, adult communication had never been one of her strong suits—Paige cleared her throat. "Maybe I will go for that walk after all."

Penny grinned. "You better take a sweater. It might be June, but it still gets pretty cold when the breeze rolls in from the ocean." She tossed one toward Paige. "And don't come back for at least an hour. You need a break before I put you to work painting."

She left the large, decrepit beach house her sister had gotten stuck with when her fiancé had walked out, and wondered what exactly she was supposed to do for the next little while as she had, for all intents and purposes, been banished from the house. If Penny seemed to think Paige needed a walk, maybe a walk was exactly what she would have. It wasn't as though she didn't like the ocean, after all. In Los Angeles they lived only a few blocks from the water and she made a point of taking Luke to the beach at least once a week.

But the water in L.A. was different than the water here. Calmer, warmer. And less laden with memories.

She wasn't going to let those memories bother her, though, she reminded herself as she descended the short flight of stairs from her sister's yard to the rocky, isolated beach. She'd promised that to herself when she'd made the decision to come to help Penny get the house ready for guests, had promised herself that she wouldn't let herself get caught up in the past.

Besides nine years was long enough to change her from the scared, insecure girl who had looked for affection in all the wrong places into a woman who knew what she wanted and how to get it.

The trick was to avoid getting so bogged down in what used to be that she forgot what was.

With that thought foremost in her mind, Paige slipped her shoes off and walked where the water met the sand. Though the dark blue water was cold—nearly frigid, really—she enjoyed the feel of it tickling her toes, licking at her ankles. The sand squished beneath her heels, then between her toes as the water receded, before her prints washed away with each new wave.

For a minute, she wished the past could be washed away as easily.

But, no, that wasn't exactly true, was it? Because if she hadn't made the mistakes she had, she wouldn't have Luke. And without him, she never would have made it after everything that happened here. After Logan had—

She cut the thought off before it could take hold. Damn this town and all the memories it evoked. In L.A. she could go weeks, months even, without thinking about him. But here, on this beach, looking out at the choppy, wind-razed Pacific it was almost impossible to keep thoughts of him at bay. Especially when she looked at Luke, here in Prospect. He looked so much like his father that here, in all of her old haunts, nearly everything he did evoked memories she would rather forget.

No matter how hard things had been, no matter how difficult those first months and years had been after she'd moved to L.A., she wouldn't change a thing. Not if changing things meant she lost even a little bit of what she'd worked so hard to give Luke.

Stability.

Security.

Unconditional love.

Three things she'd never had growing up with two parents who despised her. Three things she swore her child would never do without.

A large wave rolled onto the beach, soaking her to her knees and spraying up onto her thighs and stomach. Paige laughed, a gasping, sucking kind of sound as she tried to ignore the bone-jarring cold that had invaded at the first brush of the water. Because, though it was freezing, it felt good. Felt wonderful to throw her troubles into the surf and let them roll a little farther out to sea.

It was as she watched the ebb and flow of the waves, savoring the feel of the cold water against her skin, that Paige made a decision.

For the time she was here, for the two months she'd promised her sister she would help with the inn, she would live in the present.

She would forget the past, forget the mistakes she'd made and the hurts she'd both inflicted and received, and focus instead on the good things she had. Luke. Penny. A job she loved waiting for her in L.A. and the chance to use everything she'd learned on that job to make the eyesore her sister had bought into something truly amazing.

And when she was done... When she was done,

she would leave Prospect for good. But this time she would do it on her own terms, knowing that she had truly put the ghosts of her past to rest, once and for all.

# CHAPTER FOUR

THE DRIVE TO PENNY MATTHEWS'S beach house seemed to take forever. Even the call he'd gotten from his mother, demanding to know if the rumors she'd been bombarded with were true—was Paige Matthews back in town, *with his son*—hadn't kept the fifteen-minute drive out of town from dragging. It had been a hell of a conversation to have. After the way his mother had hung up, he wasn't altogether sure he'd ever be allowed in the door of his parents' house again. At least he'd be in good company. Between Paige, Luke, his father's ex-lovers and his sister's children, the number of people who *were* permitted to cross the threshold dwindled a little more each year.

But when he could scarcely make sense of this situation, how could he possibly explain it in a way that would appease his exacting mother? All he knew was from the moment he'd laid eyes on the boy, from the moment he'd realized that Paige had given birth to his child, every brain cell he possessed had been working on overdrive, struggling to find the right words to say to her.

He'd almost blown it at the diner earlier and he was sorry for that. The last thing he wanted to do was make his son uncomfortable. But the shock of seeing him, of knowing that his child had been alive and growing for eight years… It had been almost impossible to see past it.

At least until Paige had called him on it. She'd always been able to do that, even when they were kids. He'd start on a path he had no business going down and she would rein him in. Until the end, when she'd walked out on him, as if trying to convince him that Luke was his hadn't been worth her time. Her effort. As if the fact that she was pregnant with his child hadn't been enough to make her fight for them.

Thinking of those long-ago arguments had his emotions rising again, though he'd worked all afternoon to control them. Joni had been furious with him when he'd returned to the diner, had accused him of humiliating her in front of the whole town. Then she'd walked out.

But, honestly, he didn't know what else he'd been supposed to do. How he should have reacted to the knowledge that he had a kid and that kid's mother hadn't so much as bothered to tell him.

Doubt and a little bit of guilt twisted at the back

of his consciousness because he knew that asser-
tion wasn't strictly true, but he shoved both emotions
aside. Ignored them. She'd had ample opportunity
over the years to tell him she'd had his child. That's
what he would concentrate on when he spoke to her.
That and not losing his temper, which was going to be
a hard one, because right now he was one step away
from feeling as though his head would explode.

The only truly coherent thought he had was that
Paige had stolen his child. She had left town, pregnant with his baby, and had never bothered to contact
him again.

Had never bothered to tell him that the baby had
been born.

Had never bothered to tell him that he was a
father.

Had never bothered to send him so much as a picture on the kid's first or second or seventh birthday.

By the time he pulled up in front of the dilapidated
house, he was even more determined to settle things
between them. He wanted an explanation, now, and
he would get it even if he had to slap cuffs on Paige
and drag her into the interrogation room at the station. One way or the other, they were going to figure
this out, tonight.

He bounded up the steps and prepared to knock
hard enough to wake the dead.

"You look loaded for bear." The words were said in

a low, relaxed voice—one he recognized immediately because he'd heard the same tone from Paige innumerable times they'd been together. Her voice was a little deeper now, a little richer, but all the important elements were the same.

Whirling, he scanned the shadows cast by the single, yellow porch light until he found her, sitting on the swing, a glass of white wine dangling carelessly from one hand and a cell phone from the other.

Her short blond hair was rumpled and she was dressed in a purple tank top and a pair of ripped and faded jeans that probably cost more than he made in a month. She still smelled like lilacs. Her feet were bare and something about her small, blue-tipped toes calmed him in a way nothing else could have. Maybe because they made him remember what it had been like to be with her all those years ago, what it had been like to love her.

When they'd been together, she had always painted her toenails some mysterious color that none of the other girls would go near but that somehow drove him absolutely insane nonetheless. He'd been too stupid to realize it hadn't all been for him, that he wasn't the only guy in town she'd been showing her polish—and other things—to.

The red haze threatened to return, and he did what he could to head it off. They would get nothing accomplished if they were yelling at each other, a realization he figured Paige had come to herself some time that afternoon, if her smooth greeting was any indicator. That or the glass of wine in her hand wasn't her first.

Sinking onto the swing across from her, he didn't say anything at first. Simply looked at her. Noted all the changes and all the things that had stayed the same through the years. Suddenly he couldn't think of anything *to* say.

"Do you want a glass of wine?" Her voice was husky, sweet, and it sent shivers up his spine even as he told himself how stupid he was to respond to her. She'd lied to him, had—

"No, thanks. I'm driving."

"That's right. You're a cop now. A law-abiding citizen. I'm having a hard time reconciling the new you with the guy I used to know."

"I was always a law-abiding citizen. I only liked to pretend otherwise."

"I remember." She took a sip of her wine.

"You look good," he said.

"L.A. agrees with me. Certainly more than Prospect ever did."

Memories stretched between them, hanging on the silence like apples on a tree, ripe for the picking. He chose to ignore them, to walk past as though he wasn't suddenly starving for a taste of them. Of her.

"His name's Luke," she said quietly, when the silence got to be too much for both of them. "It's short for Lucas."

"That's a nice name."

"I think so. It was my neighbor's, when I first moved to L.A. He helped me get settled, learn my way around. He even drove me to the hospital and waited while Luke was born. I don't know what I would have done without him."

The anger surged, burning so hotly and brightly that he couldn't think past it. "You could have come to me. You could have told me you were pregnant with our child. Then I would have been the one to be there, to help you."

"Is that how you remember it?" she asked offhandedly, as if his answer meant nothing to her.

"That's how it would have been. I would have been with you every step of the way—"

"Is that so? Because the way I remember it is, I told you I was pregnant with your child and you called me a whore—right before you tossed me out of your house."

"You were sleeping with my best friend, with half the guys on the football team. How the hell was I supposed to believe the kid you were carrying was mine?"

"I wasn't sleeping with half the football team. I wasn't sleeping with anyone but you. Only you didn't want to believe that. Any more than you wanted to accept that you'd gotten me pregnant.

"Accepting responsibility for that act would have meant you couldn't live the perfect life mapped out for you. The one that mommy and daddy wanted you to live. The one that didn't include the slutty girl from the wrong side of the river."

She was breathing hard by the time she finished, her chest rising and falling with each harsh inhalation. He probably shouldn't be cheered by that fact, but it made him feel better to know that she wasn't nearly as calm about this whole thing as she pretended to be.

He didn't answer for a minute, instead turning to stare into the inky blackness that surrounded the house. Looking at her brought back too many memories, including ones of how badly he'd treated her nine years before.

But he wasn't ready to deal with those memories yet—or the words she had just flung at him. Didn't know if he'd ever be ready now that he knew she'd kept his child from him. How easy would it have been for her to return after his son was born and force him to see her and their child? No, he wasn't going to let her turn this around. She could have played things way differently all those years ago.

"Look," he said, "I know your past is something

you're ashamed of, but you can't rewrite history to—"

She stood. "Get out of here."

"What?" he asked, rising slowly so that they were face to face. Or, in this case, face to chest, since he stood about six inches taller than she did.

"You heard me. If you think you're going to come here and insult me after all these years, then you're crazy. I'm not that girl anymore, the one who was so used to being a whipping post that she took insults from everyone—including the guy who was supposed to love her. So, leave. You're not welcome here."

Though he knew there was an important message in her words, he could only handle so much at one time and his brain focused on the fact that she was kicking him out, denying him access to his son.

"You can't do this. I have rights when it comes to my son."

"You gave up those rights the day you threw me out on my ass and told me never to come back. It was the same day you told me you'd never give my bastard your name and that I should head back to the freak show because you were done slumming."

He winced, shocked at how sharp his words had been, at how they still had the power to cut like a knife, even after all these years. "I was angry," he said stiffly.

"Oh, well, whoop-de-do. Let's stop the presses.

Logan Powell was angry. Obviously, that gave you the right to do whatever you wanted. To hurt whomever you wanted."

"I think you have that backward. *You* hurt *me*. I thought I was in love with you only to find out you were sleeping with a bunch of my buddies. What the hell did you expect me to do?"

"I expected you to believe me when I told you they were lying to you, trying to get you upset."

"Why would they do that?" he demanded. "They knew how I felt about you."

"How the hell should I know? They were *your* friends. What I never understood, not then and not now, is how you could believe them so easily? You said you loved me, yet the second your friends started with their dirty insinuations, you dumped me. Dumped our child like we were nothing."

Her words hit home, a little too closely for his comfort. But at the same time, he had a hard time believing that his friends had been lying about her. Some of those guys were his best friends to this day, had stood up with him at his wedding. They knew almost everything about each other. Surely he would know if they were liars. He was a cop, for God's sake. It was his job to know those kinds of things.

Still, he was disconcerted enough by the idea that he blurted the first thing that came to his mind.

"Why wouldn't I believe them? It's not like you were a virgin when we had sex for the first time."

She reeled in shock, as if his words had been an actual physical blow to her. And maybe they had been. Her past was not something most women would be proud of. Still, he hadn't meant to hit her with it so bluntly.

But when her eyes narrowed, he realized he'd misread the signs. She wasn't hurt or upset. She was as furious as he was. "Oh. And you *were* a virgin?" she demanded. "Because I seem to remember you running around with a number of girls before me, all of whom you admitted to sleeping with."

"Yeah, but—" He bit off the words before he could dig himself in even deeper, but it was too late.

"But, what? It's different for you, because you're a guy?"

"I wasn't going to say that," he protested, wondering how the hell this whole conversation had been turned around until he was the one on the defensive.

"Then what?"

"I don't know. I mean, it's not like your past ever bothered me—"

"Oh, really? Because I figure it bothered you a hell of a lot if you were so willing to toss me out because of a few whispers from your friends."

"It wasn't just a few whispers." Completely

frustrated, he turned away from her. Walked over to the railing. Some of the overgrown bushes were visible in the dim light from the porch and he wondered vaguely if Penny and Paige had any idea what they were in for as they tried to rehab this house. It really was a disaster.

"Look, how I once felt about your past is pretty much a moot point, don't you think?" he asked. "What's important is Luke and where we go from here."

For a second he didn't think she was going to respond, but finally she sighed and said, "So, where do you see this going?"

There it was, the question he had been asking himself since he got his first glimpse of Luke that afternoon in Prospector's. He'd turned it over in his head a million times in the last ten hours, and though he still had a lot of unanswered questions—a lot of concerns and misgivings—there was one thing he was certain of. "I want to be a part of his life."

EVEN THOUGH SHE'D PREPARED herself for it, even though she'd known it was coming, the words were still a tremendous blow. How could they not be? Luke had been hers—exclusively hers—almost from the moment she'd known of his existence. The idea that she was now expected to share him with someone else—and not just anyone else, but with the man who had rejected him, rejected her, without listening to her side of the story—grated the way nothing else ever had.

Her knee-jerk reaction was to snatch up Luke and run as fast and as far away from this god-awful town as she could possibly manage. In L.A. she had friends to support her, a job that paid the bills very nicely, a kickass attorney who wouldn't let Logan within a hundred yards of Luke. It sounded really tempting.

Penny would understand. Paige would write a check to pay for the renovations then she and Luke would be free to be on their way. She was actually halfway to the door—halfway to her checkbook—when she stopped herself. After all, she'd run nine years before and what had it gotten her except a trip back to Prospect now and a closet full of old skeletons demanding to be laid to rest? If she ran now, she was afraid she'd never get another chance to reconcile with her sister.

That was the real reason she had come to Prospect, not this stupid old house, and she'd be damned if she'd let Logan steal her sister from her a second time.

She thought of Luke's face earlier, when he'd realized his father was within reach. Thought of Penny's smile when she realized that Paige was finally ready to put the past behind her, finally ready to reconnect with her after years of feeling guilty for leaving.

No, this time she wasn't going anywhere. She'd let Logan Powell run her out of town once before. She'd be damned if she'd let him do it again. Not when her son and her sister were the ones who would suffer from her inability to stick.

Though the decision was made, for what it was worth, she still couldn't bring herself to talk to Logan, to acknowledge his right to have anything to do with Luke. In her opinion, he was nothing more than a sperm donor. The fact that she was supposed to share her son with him simply because he had suddenly woken up... It didn't sit well.

The seconds stretched endlessly, ebbing and flowing like the ocean she could hear but couldn't see. The moment wasn't comfortable, not with everything still left unsaid. But it was real, alive with the fear, the uncertainty, the anger that pulsed between them and she was loath to let it slip away. It had been so long since they'd had anything real that she couldn't help savoring it, just a little.

Logan obviously didn't have any such reticence— one more sign that they weren't on the same wavelength. He cracked after only a few minutes, his voice deep and gravelly when he asked, "Are you going to say something?"

"I don't know what you want me to say." She moved to sit on the swing, pulled her legs up underneath her. Curling up was small protection, but she would take comfort wherever she could get it.

"Sure you do. You just don't want to say it."

And there he was, the old Logan, the one she used to think she knew better than anyone else on the planet. Direct, honest, a straight shooter with a wicked sense of humor.

Considering how things had ended between them, that shouldn't make her smile. But it did. God, she was so much weaker than she'd thought she was. No wonder this trip was turning into an unmitigated disaster.

"When you say you want to be a part of his life, what are we talking about here? You want to see him a few times when we're in Prospect or are you looking for something more permanent?"

"He's my son, Paige. What do you think?"

"I think it was way too easy for you to turn your back on him once and there's nothing to say you won't do it again. I'm not going to let Luke get close to you, let Luke start to love and depend on you, if you're going to toss him aside when he's not a shiny new toy anymore. He deserves better than that and I won't stand by and let you hurt him.

"So if you really want to do this thing, if you really want to open this can of worms, you'd better think long and hard about exactly how you expect this to end up. Because until you know, until you're one hundred percent certain, I'm not letting you anywhere near my son."

"You know, this whole mother-of-the-year act is getting old. I mean, it takes a lot of nerve to act like you give a shit about a kid when you lost him in a supermarket your second day in town."

The unfairness of the accusation had her defense mechanisms firing before she could think better of it. "Well, at least I knew what name to call him when I was looking for him. Which is more than you could have done."

He paled even as his mile-wide shoulders went ramrod stiff. When he spoke, his voice was low, controlled. "And whose fault is that?"

"Yours, Logan. The fault is yours."

He didn't respond and for long seconds she couldn't breathe, as if his anger had sucked up all the oxygen around her. The emotions seething between them grew into their own entity.

"We both know I could get a court order, demanding that you let me see him." Disgust flickered across his face before he locked it away.

All of the feelings she'd ever had for him—love, rage, tenderness, hate, friendship, bitterness—combined inside her until she was choking on them. Choking on the minefield of their past and the fact that he still had the ability to hurt her, even after all these years. She didn't know if she had the energy to negotiate her way around the landmines this time around. Not when so much was at stake.

"Are you threatening me?"

"Shit, Paige." He ran a hand over his face, swore again. "Of course I'm not threatening you. But I want to see my son, want to get to know him. Is that so hard for you to believe? You've deprived me of eight years of his life. I don't want to miss any more."

"I've deprived you. Is that how you see this whole thing? *Me* depriving *you?*"

"You kept my kid a secret."

"Bullshit." She was in his face now, years of pent-up anger spurring her on. "I told you I was pregnant right after I found out. I begged you to help me, to help him. Begged you to believe that I was carrying your child.

"So don't you sit here and tell me I kept him a secret. You're the one who didn't want him. You're the one who threw him away. And if you think I'm going to stand by and let you do it again because you threaten me with a custody hearing, then you're even stupider than I remember.

"You want to go to court? Fine. Bring it on, because I will be damned before I let an insensitive, egomaniacal monster like you anywhere near my son."

She turned, would have stormed inside and

slammed the door behind her, if he hadn't grabbed her elbow and whirled her around to face him.

"I'm not doing this with you, Paige. We're both too old for the drama and I'm not doing it. You might have cast yourself as the innocent victim here, but we both know the truth. Any of half a dozen guys could have gotten you pregnant. It's my bad luck that I happened to be the one who actually did."

"Well, if that's the way you feel about it, I guess we don't have anything left to talk about, do we? Because I'm not voluntarily sharing my son with anyone who refers to his existence as *bad luck*. I'll look forward to hearing from your attorney."

Wrenching her arm from his grip, she all but dove for the house. As she closed the door behind her—making sure to slide the deadbolt into place for the first time since she'd gotten there—she was deathly afraid she had just made another gigantic mistake.

## CHAPTER FIVE

"WELL, THAT CERTAINLY went well."

Caught off-guard by the sound of her sister's voice, Paige nearly jumped through the ceiling. When she finally got her heartbeat under control, she turned to find Penny leaning against the wall.

"You heard?" Paige asked disgustedly, heading into the kitchen to pour herself another glass of wine. She'd left her other glass on the porch and as she still hadn't heard Logan's truck start, there was no way in hell she was going out there to get it.

"I did. Not hard since I was deliberately eavesdropping." Penny followed her into the kitchen, puttered around a little bit and suddenly Paige found herself sitting at the kitchen table, a cup of hot chocolate and plate of chocolate chip cookies in front of her. She reached for one, took a big bite. And wished she was still a kid, when store-bought cookies really could chase her demons away.

"So, do you want to talk about it?"

"Not really."

"Let me rephrase." Penny sat across from her. "Tell me about it."

"There's not much to tell. Especially if you heard the whole conversation."

"I didn't hear the whole thing, just the last ten minutes or so." She reached for a cookie. "You'll talk to his attorney, huh?"

"I know, I know." She slumped, barely resisting the urge to bang her head against her sister's hand-carved table. "But what was I supposed to say? He threatened me with a custody hearing."

"Not to mention insulted the hell out of you. He's lucky I didn't kick his ass for that last crack of his. Asshole."

"I know, right? How could he possibly think saying that was a good idea?"

"How could he possibly think *thinking* that was a good idea?" Penny echoed. "I mean, seriously, sis, I was wrapped up in all the drama of my first year in high school, but even I knew how far gone you were over him. There's no way you were cheating on him."

Paige eyed her over the rim of her cocoa cup. "That's what you find objectionable? Not his belief that I was sleeping with *six* different guys while I was sleeping with him, but that he thought I was cheating on him at all?"

"That *is* the objectionable part. As long as you're

not involved with someone, you're allowed to sleep with whoever you want, whenever you want. The double standard is dead—and if it isn't, it should be. Who the hell is Sheriff Hot Pants to tell you differently? I can't believe he held your past against you."

Paige choked on her cocoa. *"Sheriff Hot Pants?"*

"Yeah, well, it's not like he's been sitting around pining for you." Penny held up a hand. "No offense."

"None taken." Paige let the laughter relax her shoulders a little bit. "I don't know. Part of me wonders if I didn't deserve it—"

"You *didn't* deserve it, Paige. You didn't deserve any of the things he said to you tonight and not any of the things he said to you nine years ago. So what if you'd been with other guys before him? He doesn't know what you went through as a kid, doesn't have a clue how hard it was for you to grow up in this backwater town, where everyone knew that Mom had gotten pregnant while Dad was stationed overseas. Was it any wonder you were looking for love wherever you could get it?"

"I'm not sure it was like that. I mean, yeah, my therapist tells me all my early acting out was a way to get attention, to get Dad and Mom to notice me as something other than a whipping post. But I don't know. A lot of times, when I was doing it—hooking up with some guy I didn't know that well—it didn't feel like that. It felt like a giant *screw you* to Dad, you know?"

"If anyone ever deserved to be told off, it was our father. At least by you."

"I can't say that I really blame him. Plus, he did stick around. He stayed married to Mom, put a roof over my head and food in my stomach,"

"And never let you—or anyone else—forget for a minute that you weren't his."

"Touché." She inclined her head. "Was it any wonder, then, that Logan wasn't sure I was telling the truth? Like mother, like daughter."

Penny tried to hand her another cookie. "Take it, you obviously need it. You're getting maudlin."

"Maybe I am. But I never looked at another guy the entire time I was with Logan. I loved him." She shrugged. "I didn't always feel like I deserved him—he was so smart and handsome and funny and nice, even when he was distant—but I loved him. Desperately."

"And in the end, he was the one who didn't deserve you. What a kick in the ass that must have been."

Paige laughed, but there wasn't much humor in the sound. "What am I going to do, Penny?"

"What do you want to do?"

"Lock Luke up until he's fifty. I couldn't stand if he got hurt because of mistakes that I've made."

"I keep telling you, this isn't your mistake. It's Logan's."

"Yeah, but does who's at fault really matter right now? When Luke's the one who is going to suffer if I make the wrong choice."

"You know what I think?" her sister asked, reaching across the table and grabbing on to Paige's hand. "As long as you love Luke as much as you do, as long as you're always looking out for his best interests, I don't think he *can* get hurt. Not even by Logan. Not really hurt, anyway. You love him too much to let anything happen to him and he knows it."

"But what if I can't—"

"No buts." Penny pushed back from the table, stood up. "You need a good night's sleep and a few days to mull this over without obsessing about it."

"I think that's impossible."

"But you should still try. Give yourself a chance to breathe a little. You just got here and you're in the middle of all this. When the time's right, you'll know what to do."

"Can I get a guarantee on that?"

"Absolutely. And I'll even make it a money-back one."

"Easy for you to say when there's no cash involved."

"Exactly. Now come on, I'll race you upstairs. It'll be like old times."

Penny took off and as Paige chased her upstairs—which was indeed just like old times—she couldn't help wondering if her sister was wrong. Because from where she was sitting, it looked as though no matter what decision she made, it was going to be the wrong one.

LOGAN WAS STILL SHAKING with anger when he let himself into the garage of the small house he'd bought a few streets away from downtown. Throwing his keys on the kitchen counter, he went straight through to the fridge and pulled out a beer. Twisting off the cap, he drank it down in a few quick gulps before reaching for another one.

What good had he thought would come from seeing Paige tonight? She hadn't changed one bit and he should have realized that outside the diner. He'd been insane to think that they could handle this like two rational adults. Such a thing was impossible when one of them insisted on acting like a spoiled brat.

He really didn't like the role she'd cast him in—bad guy in this whole situation. It didn't sit well with him, as he was usually the one wearing the white hat. But even as he nursed his feelings of outrage, his conscience wouldn't let him leave it at that. Instead, he kept asking himself if he really thought Paige was the only one who had behaved badly tonight.

Sure, the circumstances were stressful. Add in the fact that he was still attracted to her—wasn't that a kick in the teeth?—and the whole situation had been explosive. He was probably lucky it had gone as well as it had.

If he considered custody threats and demands for attorneys going well, that is.

Shit. He shook his head, took a long sip of his beer. How had this thing turned into such a mess? And how the hell was he going to turn it around?

He walked over to the couch and flopped on the sofa, figured he'd flip through the channels until he found a late-night show that interested him. But once he was on the couch remote in hand, he couldn't move. All he could do was replay the moment he'd realized that the boy sitting next to Paige was his son.

He couldn't believe how much the kid looked like him—he was nearly a carbon copy. He wondered what Luke had looked like as a baby. And did his best to ignore the resentment burning in his stomach. He couldn't believe he'd missed his son's birth, his first steps, first word, first tooth. Hell, Logan had missed Luke's first everything.

Logan thought of his own family, of his brother and sister-in-law and their three kids. They'd documented everything about those kids, celebrated all of the milestones and little accomplishments. Had bombarded the family with photos and videos of Jason, Courtney and Stacy until he'd thought they were going a little overboard. And yet, now that he had a son—even one he'd known nothing about—he understood. There wasn't a minute of Luke's life that he didn't want to see, wasn't a moment that he didn't want to recreate so that he could share it. And that would never happen.

He could have kicked his teenaged self's ass for being so shortsighted that he hadn't even considered the fact that, even if she had been sleeping with other guys, she'd also been sleeping with him. He should have realized that the baby she carried could have been his.

But he'd been too caught up in his anger and embarrassment to think that far ahead. Too stupid to think of all the different ways this thing could play out.

But then, *stupid* had been his middle name back then. He'd fallen for Paige despite her reputation, had cared about her despite the fact that he knew she'd been with other guys. It hadn't mattered to him then, not when he'd gotten to know who he thought was the real Paige. Nothing had mattered but being with her and he'd thought she felt the same way.

Even when he'd started hearing the rumors about her with other guys, he'd ignored them. He trusted her. She said that she loved him and that had been more than enough for him. Besides, he'd lived in Prospect long enough to know that only about one-tenth of the rumors circulating at any given time were true.

What he'd forgotten—or chosen to forget—was that most of the rumors, no matter how outlandish, had some kind of grounding in truth. So while he'd been fighting with his friends and family about her, about what kind of person she was, Paige had been making a fool of him. She'd been sleeping with half his football team and how many others?

For months after she'd left town, he'd thanked God that he'd woken up to that fact before he'd done something stupid like thrown away his plans to go to an out-of-state college in order to stay close to her. He'd been on the verge of turning down a chance to play football at the University of Washington when he'd found out the truth about her.

But now, knowing that his son had grown up without him, he wasn't so sure. If he'd never known that Paige was sleeping with his friends—had tried to sleep with his best friend—then he would have been there for Luke from the very beginning. He had loved her and would have tried to help her any way he could. And though things between them probably wouldn't have lasted—how could they have when they'd both had so much growing up to do?—that didn't matter. What mattered was finding a way to be close to the son who didn't know him as anything more than an abstract concept.

He thought of how Paige had looked sitting on that porch tonight. Her hair had glowed in the light, lending her an almost otherworldly quality. How was it that she could look like an angel and yet be so devious?

How was it that even knowing everything that he did about her, that even being angrier at her than he could ever remember being, his body still responded to her closeness?

It was a nightmare, a fiasco, one he had no idea how to free himself from. But he had to free himself, had to find a way to make things right between them. Not relationship right, because obviously that was out of the question. Just because his body was stupid enough to still find her attractive didn't mean his brain did. There was no way he was giving her a chance to rip out his heart a second time.

But that didn't mean he couldn't be polite to her. Reasonable. Adult-like. No matter how much she'd hurt him in the past, no matter how upset he was that she'd kept his kid away from him for almost nine years, he had to put it away. Not forget about it—no, he'd never forget about it. But she was right. In this situation she held most of the cards and he'd be damned if he folded and went away.

No, he needed to ante up. If that meant biting his

tongue every time he saw her, then he could do that. He could do almost anything if it meant finally getting the chance to be the father that Luke deserved. He'd always wanted kids though his wife hadn't, and finding out that he had one—while a shock—made him happier than he'd been in a long time. He wasn't walking away from this.

There hadn't been that many things in his life that had mattered to him, even fewer that he hadn't quit when they got boring or complicated. But he wasn't going to quit on Luke, on this chance to be a father. He'd waited too long for the opportunity.

So he'd spend the next few days planning, give Paige time to calm down after the fight they'd had, and then it was full speed ahead. He would find a way to connect with his son, a way to get to know Luke and be a part of his life. Anything else didn't bear thinking about.

## CHAPTER SIX

"HEY, MOM. CATCH!"

Paige looked up from the hole she was digging in time to see Luke's football soaring straight at her head. Dropping her shovel, she reached out her arms and caught it. Calling her action *catching* was a slight exaggeration for letting the ball hit her in the chest, hard, before she wrapped her arms around it.

But as she threw it to her son, she refused to dwell on her lack of football prowess. Why should she, when it was the sport she was best at? What she really hated were the spring months when Luke played baseball and expected her to practice with him. Not much on earth was worse than trying to catch that small, hard white ball—except maybe trying to hit it.

And with basketball, winter wasn't much better, she admitted as she took the ball in the chest again, certain that this time she would end up with a pretty spectacular bruise. Ignoring the pain shooting through her left breast, she tossed the ball a second time—and couldn't help the spurt of pride that came when she realized she'd spiraled it. It had been completely accidental—despite the fact that their neighbor in L.A. had taught Luke how to throw a spiral two years ago, and then had tried to teach her. She was usually an abysmal failure at it, unlike her son, who already had the arm of a future championship quarterback, or so his last coach had told her.

Didn't it just figure that she had a son who was an incredible athlete when most days it was an accomplishment if she could keep her feet from going out from under her? Definitely Logan's genes at work.

"Sweet throw!" Luke called, taking the opportunity of her obviously improved football prowess to fire a sweet spiral of his own at her. Putting her hands out—though she wasn't sure if she was trying to catch the thing or ward it off—it hit her solidly, bending back her right index finger before she fumbled and the ball fell harmlessly to the ground.

She cursed under her breath, then curled her fingers in and out numerous times, trying to determine if her eight-year-old had managed to break her finger.

Luke laughed, even as he jogged over. "Sorry, Mom. Are you okay?"

She mock glared at him. "I don't know. I'd probably be better if my kid stopped trying to kill me with a football."

"It's not murder if you willingly participate," he

answered with a smirk that was so like his father's that it took her breath away.

When she finally managed to suck air into her lungs, she answered, "Says you."

"Says anyone." He tossed the ball up in the air, spun it, caught it without even looking. Then repeated the process again and again. "So, I finished all the chores Aunt Penny gave me."

"All of them?" she asked. "Because I know how much you hate to weed—"

"All of them," he confirmed, his quick grin melting her heart as it had been doing since he was an infant. "I was even extra careful to only pull out the weeds that looked exactly like the ones she showed me."

"I'm sure her tomatoes and bell peppers will thank you for that." She waited for him to get to whatever was on his mind. It didn't take long.

"So, I was wondering …"

"Yes?"

"Can we go get ice cream? It's been four days since I've had anything with sugar in it and really, Mom, I can only eat so many of Aunt Penny's whole-wheat pancakes with germs before going nuts."

Paige laughed. "Wheat germ, kid. Not germs. Wheat germ."

"Yeah, well, they taste pretty germy. Come on, Mom. Please?" He batted his eyes at her and she felt herself cave, even though she knew exactly what he was doing.

"Oh, wow, look at you. Bringing out the big guns, huh?"

"I wouldn't do that…Mommy." He looked practically angelic when he said it, his smile so smooth and bright that she had to blink to avoid being blinded.

Again, she couldn't help wondering how she'd ended up with such an amazing, wonderful kid. Sure, his coloring and athletic abilities came from his rat of a father, but she didn't have a clue where the rest of him came from. A natural born charmer, he could talk anyone into anything—even her, and she was well-known at work for being about as far from a pushover as someone could get.

She shuddered to think what would happen when the kid got a little older. She was going to have to invest in a good air horn to keep the girls away.

"I'll tell you what. Why don't you help me finish planting this tree and then we'll both go inside and get cleaned up? We can try to talk Aunt Penny into going into town for dinner. If you eat all your vegetables, I'll take you for ice cream."

"Sure. No problem."

She narrowed her eyes at the easy acquiescence. "French fries do *not* count as a vegetable."

"Aw, Mom."

"You can *aw, Mom* me all you want. That's the

deal. Vegetables—preferably green—in exchange for ice cream. Take it or leave it."

Luke paused, considering. "Two scoops?'

"Of vegetables? Absolutely."

"*Moooooooom*. I meant ice cream."

"Oh. You did? I thought you were anxious for a full plate of asparagus."

He made a gagging noise. "Broccoli in exchange for two scoops of ice cream—strawberry and cookies-and-cream. That's my final offer."

"Your final offer, huh?"

"Yep. Take it or leave it."

She reached out and tweaked his nose. "I guess I'll take it, then."

"Woo-hoo!" he exclaimed, going up on tiptoes to brush a kiss across her cheek. "Thanks, Mom! You're the best."

Paige pretended to buff her nails against her shirt. "I try."

"You succeed! Now come on." He yanked at her. "Let's get the tree."

"We need to finish the hole first. It's not deep enough for the root ball."

"So what?"

"So what? It won't do us any good to plant the tree if we don't make sure it's going to survive."

Luke rolled his eyes. "All right, all right." He reached

for the shovel and began digging enthusiastically, a huge grin on his face.

When they were finally finished, she herded him to the house for a shower. With an almost nine-year-old's typical aversion to any water he couldn't swim in, Luke mumbled and grumbled about that part of their bargain all the way to the house. But once they got inside, he made a beeline—whooping and hollering—for the only working shower in the place.

"What's that all about?" Penny asked as she—and her do-it-yourself plumbing manual—came out of the downstairs bathroom.

Paige shook her head at the sight of her beautiful sister dressed in painter's overalls, and covered in something she'd rather not know the identity of. Penny—and her stubborn determination to do almost all the work at the inn by herself—was the primary reason they only had one working bathroom at the moment.

"I promised him we'd all have dinner and ice cream in town, provided it was okay with you."

"Are you kidding me? I'm all about ice cream."

"And germy pancakes."

"Of course— Wait. What kind of pancakes?"

Paige explained Luke's take on wheat germ and they both laughed. "I guess I still need to work on that recipe before I serve it to the guests," Penny said, crossing to the kitchen to wash her hands.

"I like them."

"Yeah, but you like almost anything. You've got an industrial-strength stomach."

"Hey. My stomach has served me well through the years."

"I know. Remember that time we climbed the trees in Old Man Witherspoon's orchard and gorged on cherries? You were the only one who didn't get sick."

"I do remember. And it was a good thing, since I had to get all of you home."

"I thought Mom was going to kill you for letting me get so sick."

"Not that that was anything unusual. Mom always wanted to kill me."

An awkward silence descended and Paige waited for all the platitudes Penny had voiced through the years. Waited for her sister to defend their mother, as she always had. Waited for her to ask when Paige was planning to stop by to see their parents since she'd been in town nearly a week and hadn't gone near the house they had both grown up in.

But Penny didn't say anything for the longest time, so long that Paige started to head upstairs, figuring Luke was probably done with his shower. She was halfway to the staircase when Penny finally spoke.

"They were wrong."

Shock ricocheted through Paige and for a second she was sure she had heard incorrectly. "What?"

"To treat you the way they did. They were wrong. Terribly wrong. Mom especially. I never understood why she felt the need to punish you for her mistakes."

Pain ripped through Paige, sharp little shards of glass that embedded themselves in her bloodstream, leaving small, bleeding wounds behind wherever they touched. "It's no big deal."

"It's a very big deal. The way they treated you was awful. I'm sorry I never stuck up for you. I was afraid of making things worse."

"It wasn't your job to stick up for me. I was capable of doing that myself." But it would have been nice not to have felt so alone all the time, not to have felt as though it was her against the world. Maybe she wouldn't have—

Things were what they were and her past was what it was. Bemoaning it now wasn't going to change anything. She hadn't spoken to her mother—or the man who had raised her—since she'd left town, pregnant and alone, all those years ago.

"No. It *was* my job. And I failed at it. I should have opened my mouth."

The pain grew sharper, and Paige knew if she didn't get out of there quickly, she was going to say something she regretted. Penny might not understand what her parents had done to Paige, but she still loved them. Confessing what Paige thought of them wouldn't help anything.

"Look, Luke is going to be down any minute. We need to get ready to go to town—"

It was as if Penny hadn't heard her. "I didn't say anything then, but I learned from my mistake. I'm not going to keep my mouth shut again when saying something could change how things play out."

The resolve in her sister's voice stopped Paige in her headlong flight upstairs. "What are you getting at?"

"I know I said the other night that Logan was a complete asshole—and I'm sticking by that assessment. But, Paige, have you noticed that Luke has made an excuse every day to go into town? Today it's ice cream. Yesterday it was a wheel for his skateboard. The day before it was a trip to the library to get books."

"He's a little bored. It's very different here than it is in Los Angeles and—"

"He's not bored. He's looking for a chance to bump into Logan again."

Icy shock replaced the pain of a few minutes before. "What?"

"He knows his dad is in town, knows he works in town, and is doing everything he can to get there to see him. He wants to meet his father."

Even as she opened her mouth to deny her sister's words, Paige couldn't help wondering if Penny was right. Hadn't she noticed Luke's spectacular disinterest in his skateboard after she'd bought him the new wheel—it still sat in the bag in the corner of their room where he'd left it after they'd gotten home yesterday. And hadn't she wondered why he hadn't asked for ice cream one of the days they were in town? It wasn't like Luke to pass up an opportunity to ask for his favorite treat. Unless…

Unless he'd been planning this whole thing all along.

Unless he had been making excuses to go into town every day in an effort to run into Logan.

Unless he really did want to meet his father.

Idly, she wondered what tomorrow's excuse was going to be.

When Luke hadn't brought Logan up after that first day, she'd thought he'd changed his mind. That maybe he hadn't been all that impressed with his father after seeing him. But now she had to admit that her sister was probably right. She'd been so caught up in her anger, so caught up in her resentment of Logan, that she hadn't seen it.

So much for being a good mother. Her son was going through a crisis and she hadn't even noticed that anything was wrong. A sense of failure invaded her, not for the first time since she became a mother, but for the first time in a while. It had been years since she'd felt this down, this helpless, this wrong.

The question was what was she going to do about it?

Logan's words reverberated in her mind, his mention of court orders. His implication that she was a bad mother. His threats to take Luke from her.

He couldn't do that—she wouldn't let him. She had a really good job in L.A., probably made more money than he did, if it came down to going to court.

She wasn't an unfit mother. She'd spent the past eight years making sure that Luke never felt the way she had growing up, that he never believed for a second that he was anything but an incredible gift to her. She might have only been seventeen when she'd gotten pregnant with him, but he hadn't ruined her life. He'd given her a life.

Without him, she didn't know if she would have had the strength to walk away from her parents and their viciousness. She'd left because she knew she couldn't bring a baby into the same toxic atmosphere that she had grown up in.

And getting pregnant had given her a whole lot of insight, very quickly, into what Logan really thought of her. She'd been such a fool at seventeen, had convinced herself that the things she'd done to get attention in the past didn't matter to him. What a joke that had turned out to be.

Because while she'd been spinning all kinds of romantic daydreams about him, he'd been like all the other guys—using her to scratch an itch. She'd believed that he loved her as much as she loved him only to find out that he didn't love her, and that he believed all the stupid rumors flying around.

She was used to that kind of stuff from her parents, but Logan had seemed different. He had held her, whispered his dreams to her, told her that they would be together forever. Finding out it had all been a lie, finding out that he considered her nothing more than trash, had shattered her.

She'd gotten over it—of course she had. He might have ripped her heart out once, but she'd spent the past nine years repairing it, and building a wall around her heart that he could never breach.

Which is why she could do this. Why she could call him up and ask him if he wanted to meet them for ice cream. She would pretend that those long-ago nights and promises had happened to someone else.

If Luke wanted to meet his father, wanted to try to build a relationship with him, then she wasn't going to stand in his way—even if it ripped her apart. Her son meant everything to her. She'd always thought that she would brave the gates of hell itself for him. So surely she could handle making nice for a few hours with the man who had made his existence possible.

Right?

Absolutely, she assured herself as she reached for the small phone book Penny kept in the cabinet beneath the phone. And if she had to superglue a smile on her face before she met him, then so be it. Luke was worth it. He was worth anything.

## CHAPTER SEVEN

TWO AND A HALF HOURS LATER, Paige wasn't so sure. Not about her kid being worth everything because, hey, he totally was. But about letting Logan into his life. When they'd arranged to meet at the ice cream parlor at eight o'clock, Logan had sounded thrilled at the chance to finally meet his son, which was why she'd told Luke over dinner that he would be meeting his father.

Her son had nearly jumped out of his chair in excitement, had babbled nonstop through the meal about what it would be like to finally know his dad. He'd bombarded her with questions about Logan, questions he'd never asked before but that must have been simmering inside him for quite a while to come out in the well-organized barrage that they had.

She'd answered what she could, but she hadn't kept tabs on Logan through the years. She didn't know how long he'd been back in town, didn't know what he'd been doing in the years since she'd left. She'd made it a point not to know.

Penny had stepped in and answered some of the

questions—had told him about his dad being a homicide detective in Seattle, about the fact that he'd
been married for a while. As Paige had listened to
her sister relate her somewhat sketchy knowledge of
Logan's life, she'd been overwhelmed by sadness.

How awful was it that this man, who had once
meant everything to her—who she had made a baby
with—had turned into someone she didn't know anything about? He'd given her a child, which was the
most intimate gift one person could give another,
and yet they meant nothing to each other. Less than
nothing.

But now, well over an hour later, her sadness had
turned to annoyance. She glanced at the clock on
her cell phone again, saw that seven minutes had
passed since she'd last checked it, which meant that
Logan was now twenty-three minutes late. So much
for being anxious to finally meet his son.

Luke had rushed them through the last half of
dinner, determined not to be late for his date with
his father. The result was that they'd arrived about
ten minutes early, which meant that she had had to
sit here for over thirty minutes, watching as her son
jumped every time the door opened.

Watching as his beautiful face lit with hope every
time the bell jangled.

Watching as his shoulders slumped a little more
with each person who hadn't been his father.

To be fair, Logan had called right around eight o'clock, to tell them he was running late—the life of a police officer, he'd said with what sounded like a grimace. She appreciated the call, appreciated that Logan had agreed to meet them on such short notice. But watching her son's painful excitement was hard to bear.

Even as she told herself that Logan would be here, that he'd called, a part of her was stressed at the idea of him standing up their son. Maybe she should have more faith in him, but it wasn't as though he'd dropped everything to be here with Luke. Plus, it wasn't as though she didn't know Logan's modus operandi, didn't know that he couldn't be depended on. Couldn't be trusted.

Tonight was a perfect example. She always dropped everything when Luke was involved. Logan, who had claimed to be so fascinated with his son, couldn't even make it to an ice cream parlor on time—with two hours' notice. It didn't bode well for the father-son future. And while part of her was excited that Logan might only be a small part of her son's life for a little while, the mother in her wanted to kick her own ass for agreeing to this to begin with.

If Luke got hurt, she was going to plow her fist into Logan's face and to hell with getting arrested for assaulting an officer. It would be worth it, especially since she'd wanted to do it for nine long years.

"I say we give him seven more minutes and then get the hell out of this place," Penny whispered. "If Luke jumps one more time, I swear I'm going to cry."

Paige knew exactly how she felt. Watching her son wipe his sweaty palms on his jeans, watching him smile anxiously, was killing her. Logan had better show up—she didn't think either of them could go through this again.

"He'll be here, Mom." Luke's voice was low and small, but had the same underlying determination he had faced life with for all eight years of his existence. "I'm sure of it."

She wanted to ask how he was so sure, but knew that that would only make him more nervous, so she kept her mouth shut. Instead she started preparing a speech about why his father might not have been able to make it—police officers are important people, emergencies, et cetera. She prayed she wouldn't have to use it.

The bell attached to the door jangled yet again and Paige felt her entire body grow tense. Though she wasn't looking in that direction, somehow she knew that this time it was Logan—even before she saw her son's face. There was something about him, something about being in the same room with him, that seemed to suck up all of the air around her.

"Mom! He's coming over here!" Luke practically

jumped up and down in his chair. "What should I say?"

"You could start with hello."

The look he threw her told her how totally lame he found the answer, but she didn't have a better one. She wasn't sure what she was going to say to Logan either.

But whatever it was, she'd better think of it quickly. Because the look on his face said he wasn't leaving here without some answers, one way or the other.

And wasn't that just typical? What had she learned nine years ago, growing up in this hellhole of a town? That no good deed goes unpunished? It looked like tonight that expression was going to fit to a T.

With an inward sigh, she put her game face on. And wondered when things were going to get a little easier. She was so tired of fighting the entire world.

LOGAN'S HEART WAS BEATING way too fast as he crossed the small ice cream parlor. How sad was it that, even in Seattle, he could go into tense situations without breaking a sweat, but facing Luke—and Paige—had him so freaked out he could barely form a coherent thought.

He'd tried to be on time—had done everything he could to get here before eight o'clock. But at 7:15, a domestic violence call had come through and with Riley, his deputy on duty, tied up on a robbery case across town, he'd had no choice but to take it himself.

Wasn't it typical? Not much happened in Prospect in the months and weeks before the tourists showed up en masse. Yet it didn't escape his notice that the past week had been loaded with unexpected complaints and situations that had required police intervention. It was as if the town itself was conspiring to keep him away from Paige. And from his son.

But that didn't matter now. Nothing did but making a good first impression on his son, though he didn't have the foggiest idea how to do that.

In the end, Paige broke the ice for them. "Hi, Logan. How are you?"

He focused on her like the lifeline she was—with every ounce of concentration he had in his body. "I'm fine. Sorry I'm late. If there was any way I could have gotten here on time…"

His voice trailed off and he soaked in every detail of her. She looked good tonight—really good. Dressed in jeans that hugged her abundant curves and a hot pink knit shirt that showed off her glowing skin while also cupping her breasts, it was hard to imagine she was the mother of an eight-year-old son. *His* eight-year-old son.

For a minute, he was transported to high school, when they'd hung out here and talked about how much they wanted out of this town. He had never minded Prospect, but Paige had wanted out with a single-minded intensity that had bordered on obsession. He had gone along with her because—well, because he hadn't wanted to lose her. In the end, nothing had worked out the way they'd planned, and even after all these years it was still a kick in the ass that they'd both gotten out, but it hadn't been together.

"It's okay, Dad. Mom and I talked about how important your job is and how sometimes you can't get away."

Logan froze at the sound of the nervous little voice, a million emotions and thoughts rushing through him at the same time. His son had called him *Dad*—something that had seemed a hundred years off even a week ago. Paige had made excuses for him—something he wouldn't have guessed possible based on her animosity towards him. The entire ice cream parlor was looking at them, eavesdropping— something he should be used to, but that he totally resented now, as he met his son for the first time. This was personal, and no one else's business but his, Paige's and Luke's.

Knowing he couldn't avoid it any longer—not wanting to avoid it, despite his own all-consuming nervousness—Logan turned to his son. And was struck again by how beautiful he was. Luke's silver eyes were alive with intelligence and mischief and his little face was glowing, much as his mother's did, as if he was lit up from the inside by some vibrance, that the rest of the world could only guess at.

"Thanks—" His voice broke and he cleared his throat, tried again. "Thanks a lot, Luke. I appreciate that. I've been really anxious to meet you."

"I've been anxious to meet you, too."

An awkward silence spread as Logan struggled for something else to say and he threw Paige a look of desperation, though he didn't expect her to rescue him. He figured letting him anywhere near Luke was the limits of her beneficence.

But she surprised him. "Luke's been waiting for you to get his ice cream. Why don't you take him up to the counter and let him pick something out?"

He latched on to the suggestion like the lifeline it was. "Absolutely. What's your favorite flavor?"

"I *loooooooove* strawberry ice cream."

"Me, too." Instinct had him holding his hand out, and his heart tripped when Luke unhesitatingly slipped his small hand into his. "It's my favorite."

"Cool! I also like chocolate chip." Luke sent him a cagey look. "Can I get a scoop of each? I ate all my vegetables at dinner."

He started to say "sure, of course," he could have three scoops and a milkshake if he wanted—he could have anything—but remembered Paige at the last second. He glanced at her for permission, then felt as though he'd been hit in the stomach by a sledge-hammer. The way she was smiling at Luke—as if the sun rose and set on their son—turned her from merely pretty to absolutely gorgeous. It made her nearly incandescent and he felt an unwanted tug low in his belly as he remembered a time when she had looked at him that way.

It had been the happiest time of his life—until he'd learned that he wasn't the only one on the receiving end of her looks and kisses. That had nearly killed him, especially since he'd spent most of his life watching his father fool around on his mother. When it had happened to him, it had hit entirely too close to home.

"Since we had a deal, you can have two scoops. But that's all. And don't think it's going to be a regular thing, mister."

"Awesome! Thanks, Mom." Luke looked up at him. "Is that okay, Dad? I mean, can I get two scoops like Mom says?"

"Of course." He glanced at Paige, his eyes drawn to her like metal to a strong magnet. "What can I get for you and Penny?"

"Nothing for me," Penny drawled, standing. "In fact, I think I'm going to head out. I've been up since five this morning. You don't mind giving my sister and nephew a ride home tonight, do you, Logan?"

"No. Of course not."

"But—" Paige latched on to her sister's hand. "I thought we were going to—"

"I know. But I'm tired, sis. You understand, don't you?"

Paige didn't answer, but it didn't take many of his investigating skills to pick up on the silent battle of wills being waged between the two sisters. Penny must have won, though, because Paige finally said, "Okay. I'll see you in a little while." There was such disgust in the words and inflection, not to mention an implied threat, that he would have felt bad for Penny if he hadn't felt so insulted at Paige's obvious reluctance to have anything to do with him.

It was stupid, especially considering both their past and their last interaction, but there it was. He was obviously an idiot.

As Penny exited, he was left alone with his son and his—Paige. He didn't know what else to call her at that point. "So, can I get you anything?"

"Come on, Mom. Decide." Luke seemed to dance with impatience beside him.

"Okay, okay. You could give a woman a chance, you know." She grinned at her son, then turned to Logan, including him in her amusement. "I'll take a scoop of butter pecan, please."

The tug in his belly became a hit from a sledge-hammer as he realized how much he still liked being smiled at by Paige. A little tug of attraction pulled at him, but he ignored it. Concentrated instead on how good it felt to be included—even for a while—in the obvious affection between mother and son.

"Sure. All right, Luke. The sooner we get that ice cream, the sooner we can dig in."

"That's what I've been trying to tell you."

Paige laughed and Logan laughed with her. He couldn't help it. Luke was too damn adorable for words.

A few minutes later they were sitting together, their ice cream in front of them. Luke dived into his like a starving man and Logan watched him with amazed indulgence.

"He can really put it away," he commented to Paige as Luke shoved a particularly large bite of chocolate chip into his mouth.

"You have no idea. I'm already dreading the high school years." But she reached out and tapped Luke on the forearm. "Let's show your dad that you weren't raised in a barn, hmm?"

Luke grinned. "Sorry, Mom. But this is the best ice cream ever."

"It is," Logan agreed. "I used to dream about it when I lived in Seattle."

Luke looked scandalized. "They don't have ice cream in Seattle?"

"They do. But none this good."

"Oh." He shoveled another bite into his mouth. "I can believe that. This is really good."

Silence reigned for a few seconds, as Logan struggled to find a new topic. "So, what grade are you going into in the fall?"

"Third grade. Which is totally cool, because I don't have to be on the baby side of the school anymore. Third, fourth and fifth graders get a whole separate wing."

"That is cool. Where do you go to school?"

"I go to Seattle Prep. It's really great, except for the fact that we have to wear dorky uniforms. None of the other kids who live near me have to wear uniforms to school, which stinks. Especially since, even on free dress days, we never get to wear jeans."

"Rose wears a uniform to school as well, Luke, and she lives right next door to us."

"That's because she goes to my school, too, so that so doesn't count. Besides, she's a girl." He said the last as if it was a cross between a particularly heinous breed of insect and mass murderer.

"Hey, I'm a girl, you know." Paige infused her voice with mock outrage.

"But you're a mom."

"Oh. Is there an exemption from total girl uncoolness if you're a mom?"

Luke flashed a grin, and for the first time Logan

realized he had his mother's dimple at the left corner of his mouth. "There is if you're my mom."

"Lucky me."

"Exactly."

Logan was struck anew by the easiness between Paige and her son. From all appearances, she was an incredible mother—something that didn't jive with his preconceived notions about her. In fact, when he'd heard that she'd lost her kid in the supermarket, his first thought had been, of course. What could you expect from a woman who had come from the kind of house Paige had? A woman who spent a good portion of her life on her back?

Now, watching her with Luke made those thoughts feel disloyal—no matter how true they might be. Add in the fact that she was obviously doing well enough to afford to send their kid to private school, and he felt as though he was seeing a whole different side to Paige Matthews. A side that he couldn't help respecting, despite everything that had already passed between them.

The time seemed to fly, as Logan concentrated on learning as much as he could about his son and Paige. The more he learned, the more impressed he was with both of them. Yet, in direct juxtaposition, the more his resentment of Paige also grew.

She'd deprived him of his son for eight years, deprived him of getting to know Luke as he changed from a baby to a toddler to the fun, amazing boy sitting in front of him now. He wanted those years back, wanted them with a vengeance, and it physically hurt that no matter how hard he wished, he would never, ever have them.

By the time he pulled his police cruiser in front of Penny's house, his insides were a seething mass of emotions that he wasn't sure how to sort out. Hell, he wasn't sure he *could* sort them out. The only thing he knew for certain was that he wanted to see Luke again—and soon.

"You know, there's a carnival coming to town next week. Do you want to go with me?" he asked his son as Luke crawled out of the car.

His face lit up. "Yeah! Will it have rides?"

"Of course."

"And games? I love to shoot water into the clown's mouth and try to win a prize."

"I can't guarantee that they'll have that game, but I know that there will, indeed, be games."

"Cool. I want to try and throw a ball into the goldfish bowls. Mom won me a fish that way last year, but he died a few months ago. I still have all his stuff, though, so a new fish would be good."

Logan laughed—he couldn't help himself. Not at his son, but at the happiness zinging its way through his system. "I'll do my best to win you a fish." And if he couldn't, then he'd stop by the pet store in town.

Frank would set him up with a whole aquarium full of fish if that's what Luke wanted.

"Excellent. I'll see you later, Dad."

Paige cleared her throat. "Aren't you forgetting something?" she asked her son.

"Oh, right. Thanks for the ice cream, Dad. It was great." Then he did the most amazing thing. He reached in through Logan's open window and gave him a big hug before turning and running up the steps and into the house.

If his heart hadn't already been on the verge of exploding, that hug would have done him in. At least until he turned to Paige and realized she looked like she'd been sucking on a particularly sour lemon.

## CHAPTER EIGHT

"I WOULD APPRECIATE IT if you asked me about taking Luke out before you invite him somewhere," Paige said after they had both climbed out of the car, her tone as prim and proper as any schoolmarm's.

Still buzzing on the hug he'd gotten from his son— *his son*—it took Luke a few seconds to comprehend that Paige was angry at him. Again. Once it sunk in, he felt an answering flare of annoyance inside him, but beat it down. No use both of them being upset— he didn't need a replay of the other night, when they had parted only after hurling words such as *lawyer* and *custody suit* at each other.

"You're right. I had such a good time with him tonight that I didn't think. I'm sorry."

Paige froze, as if his apology was the last thing she was expecting to hear. But it obviously mollified her as she relaxed, took a deep breath. "He had a really great time tonight, too."

"You think so?" He hated that he sounded so anxious, as if he was in search of validation. But to be honest, he was.

"Are you kidding me? Luke's a talker, don't get me wrong. But he surpassed himself tonight. I'm shocked he let you get a word in edgewise."

"I liked listening to him. He's a great kid." He paused, then said what he'd been thinking since arriving at the ice cream parlor. "You've done a great job with him."

"Despite losing him in the grocery store?" There was no defensiveness in her tone, only an underlying amusement that had him returning the smile.

"Despite that. After meeting Luke, I guess I could see how it might be hard to keep track of all that energy."

She laughed. "That's an understatement. But usually I do a better job of it."

Silence descended and he cleared his throat. "I should go."

"Probably."

Neither of them moved. He didn't know why he didn't climb in the car and drive away—it would be the smart thing to do. The right thing to do. But with the moonlight casting Paige's face in shadows and the light wind bringing the scent of lilacs—her scent—straight to him, they might still have been teenagers in her parents' driveway. For a minute, he wanted to return to that time when he could have pulled her into his arms and kissed her the way he was suddenly aching to do. Wanted to go back to when they were both too young and too stupid to realize that the future wasn't necessarily theirs for the taking.

Of course, if he could go back, he would probably shake the hell out of himself, warn himself that nothing and no one was really what it seemed—especially not the girl he had loved above all else. But that eighteen-year-old kid would never have believed him, not when he had been so completely starstruck.

How many times had he ignored the warnings his parents, his friends, her own father had delivered to him?

How many times had he told himself that he was different—that what they had together was different?

Too many.

And she'd made a fool of him in front of his friends and teammates and he hadn't been able to see past it.

Or maybe it was more like he hadn't *wanted* to see past it. Though he'd told her, and himself, that her past hadn't mattered to him, he'd known that that wasn't strictly true. He hadn't liked that she'd had sex with so many people, certainly more than he had at the time. Most days he'd avoided thinking about it, but at strange moments the numbers had come back to him—along with the fear that one of those others had been better than him. A better listener, a better boyfriend, a better lover.

There was a part of him that had almost been relieved when his friends had told him what she was doing. It had given him the excuse he'd needed to get away from Paige, and the feelings of inadequacy he didn't know what to do with. He'd spent most of his life at the top—of the football team, the class rankings, the boyfriend scale. Playing second fiddle hadn't come easily to him.

His thoughts made him shift uncomfortably, had him blurting out his intentions instead of working up to them. "I want to see Luke again."

"I kind of figured that when you invited him to go to the carnival with you."

"The carnival doesn't come to town until next week—I want to see him before that."

Her smile faded, her face growing wary. "All right. When do you want to see him?"

"Every day. I have a lot of catching up to do and I don't want to wait any longer than I already have to get started."

"You don't want to wait? Funny how this all keeps coming back around to what you want, Logan."

"Don't start, Paige. We agreed I'd have a chance to get to know Luke."

"Getting to know him is one thing, spending every moment of your free time with him is another. I mean, sure, it's great to be you. You waltz in here after eight years and take him for ice cream and to the carnival and I'm sure you'll think of a lot of other great places to go in the next few weeks—"

"What's wrong with that? I want him to enjoy himself, to be happy."

"Well, good for you that you want to make Luke happy. But children's happiness doesn't always come from eating buckets of sugar and throwing up on rides. It comes from structure, from a schedule. From knowing he can count on you to be there to make sure breakfast is on the table or that his teeth get brushed or to read him a book at bedtime."

"I want to do all that, too."

"Do you, really? Because it's not fun, Logan. Being a parent isn't all fun and games. It can't be. And I think you've got a lot of nerve offering up nonstop good times at him without even talking to me about what *I* want for him."

Logan's eyes narrowed, but she was too caught up in her diatribe to care. "Yes, he's your biological son. Big deal. I'm the one who's raised him, who's walked the floors with him when he was teething and slept next to his bed when he was sick. I'm the one who's sat through hours of homework and projects and really bad piano recitals. And I'm the one who is going to have to be there in two months, when we leave Prospect and Luke suddenly realizes that his dad isn't interested in being anything more than a present on his birthday and at Christmas."

She flung the last accusation at him and it hung between them for long seconds. Paige could tell from the stiffness in Logan's shoulders that she'd gone too far, but she couldn't bring herself to care. All the resentment she'd carried around was pouring out of her. All the times she'd sat up with her son, alone, worried that she was doing something wrong. Worried that she wasn't doing enough. Worried that... just worried. Worried, worried, worried. Sometimes she'd felt it was a full-time job on its own.

"You want to tell me where you got the idea that I'm not in this for the long haul?" Logan asked through gritted teeth. "I want to be a part of Luke's life."

"Well, goody for you. But I think it'd be better if we took things slowly."

"I don't want to take anything slowly! I've already missed too damn much of his life, Paige. I want to be a father to him."

"I can see that. But, like I said, being a father is about more than taking the kid for ice cream or on a few rides."

"That's what I'm talking about—why I want to see him every day. So that I can get to know him, learn everything there is to know about him."

"And break his heart when he's learned to depend

on you?" The words came out of nowhere, but once they were spoken, Paige wouldn't have retracted them even if she could. Not when they so accurately summed up how she felt about him and what he'd done to her.

Logan had betrayed her nine years ago, had chosen his friends over her. How was she supposed to believe he wouldn't do the same thing with their son?

Everything had started out great with them, too. When Logan had been with her, really with her, she'd felt as though she was the center of his universe. And when he'd cut her out of his life, he'd done it as absolutely. It was as if he had forgotten all about her, and any argument she had tried to make had fallen on deaf ears. After a few weeks, she'd figured out that she had, quite simply, ceased to exist for him.

The pain had taught her well. She couldn't count on anyone else to take care of her or make her happy. And she damn sure couldn't count on anyone to take care of her son for her. Luke was her responsibility and she would do what she thought was best for him.

"Why are you so convinced I'm going to do the wrong thing by him?"

"Why wouldn't I be? What have you done to make me think otherwise? You were late for your first meeting with him, proving to both Luke and

me that your job is more important to you than he'll
ever be."

"I'm a small-town sheriff." His voice was quiet,
cold. "Sometimes emergencies come up. I can't do
anything about that."

"No one's asking you to, Logan. But Luke's a kid.
He doesn't understand all that. He's a little boy who
wants a father."

"I know that. That's why I'm trying to be one for
him."

"Yeah, for now. But what happens when you get
bored or busy or don't want to see him anymore?
What happens when he does or says something that
doesn't fit your order of the universe and you cut him
out? He won't understand—"

"That isn't going to happen."

"How do I know that? You got rid of me when you
thought I didn't fit your perfect image. And you've
lost interest in nearly everything you've ever done
in your life. Me, your football scholarship, being a
homicide detective in Seattle, your marriage. Name
one thing you've stuck to when things got tough and
maybe I'll reexamine my opinion of you."

His eyes narrowed. "None of that happened the
way you're making it sound."

"Oh, really? So you didn't walk away from me the
second the gossip got too hot for you to handle? You
didn't quit the Huskies football team the second you

got injured, though everyone said you would be able to play again?"

"He's my son. I'm not going to quit on him."

"You already did, before he was even born. Why will this time be any different?"

"You're being irrational, Paige, borrowing trouble where there isn't any. But what should I expect from a woman who can rewrite history any way she likes it?"

"I'm not the one rewriting history, Logan. You're the one who only sees what he wants."

"How did I get to be the *only* bad guy in this situation? We were both immature, we both made mistakes. If you hadn't lied to me, we wouldn't be here now."

"I never lied to you!"

"Bullshit. Now you're not remembering clearly. You used to lie to everyone, all the time, about everything. About where you were and who you were with and what you were doing."

"But I never lied to you—"

"Why? Because I was so special? Give me a break. At the time, I put it down as your defense mechanism, your way of not letting people see how easily you could get hurt. But you have to admit, a history of not telling the truth made it a little difficult for me to believe you when push came to shove. After all, you are the one who cheated on me. And you're the one who got pregnant, despite the fact that we used birth control. So how was I supposed to believe you when you told me that you were carrying my kid?"

"Because I *wasn't* cheating on you. Because I didn't get pregnant on my own. Because I loved you and you said you loved me and I thought that meant something. Because you owed me—and our child— the benefit of the doubt before you simply cut us out of your life. If you really thought I was lying to you, then you owed me the chance to prove you wrong."

The bewilderment and hurt reared up again, and not for the first time Paige cursed her decision to come here. She and Luke had a good life in L.A., one she'd worked very hard for and one that she enjoyed very much. When she was there, she didn't think about the past. Or at least, didn't dwell on might-have-beens. Things were good and that was enough.

But here, where everything had started, things were a million times more complicated. Not only because Logan was here, demanding to be a part of Luke's life, but because he resurrected feelings in her that she'd thought were long dead. Feelings of inadequacy and hurt and betrayal and, yes, even long- ing. Maybe not for him, but for what had once been. For what the seventeen-year-old Paige had wanted to be.

It was an awkward place for her to be in, especially when she had a child she needed to protect.

The seconds ticked by and she watched Logan, who seemed lost in a world of his own as he paced their little stretch of driveway. Though his face was shadowed, his body language said he was as disturbed as she was. She was sorry for that—sorry that she had been the one to blast his good mood out of the water. At the same time, she couldn't regret asking the questions she needed answered.

"Look," Logan finally said. "It's obvious we have very different interpretations of what happened back then. You're furious because I cut you out. I'm livid because you kept my son away from me."

"I didn't—"

"You did. You could have gotten in touch with me after he was born, could have demanded a paternity test to prove that he was my child."

"Why should I have to do that? I told you he was yours, begged you to believe me. And after he was born—when I was still in the hospital—I had Penny call you and tell you about him. You hung up on her."

"I didn't think—"

"Do you think I care what you thought? Do you think I really give a damn about that? I did what I could to let you know about your son. I have absolutely no guilt on that front. And I am not going to stand here and listen to you try to weasel your way out of your own culpability. You were wrong. And if you can't accept that, I don't think you need to be a part of Luke's life."

He got in her face then. "Don't even think about keeping my son from me."

"I don't respond well to threats. You keep that in mind."

"Neither do I. You might keep that in mind, as well."

She refused to give him the satisfaction of retreating, so she stayed where she was. Breathing the same air Logan was. Looking into eyes that were so like their son's it made her heart catch in her chest.

Was she being unreasonable? she wondered for the first time as she saw the pain and confusion in his expression. Was her desire to protect her son making her see phantoms where there weren't any?

She didn't know how long they stood that way, the past yawning between them like an abyss. But as the seconds turned into minutes, she became aware of a new charge in the air—one that had nothing to do with sorrow and anger and everything to do with the connection between them.

Logan leaned in a little closer and she knew she wasn't the only one affected by their proximity. He was breathing fast and hard and the heat pouring off him warmed her, despite the wind from the ocean.

He bent his head, his face getting even closer to hers, and for one, wild heartbeat, she thought he was going to kiss her.

Her heart jumped, her blood pounded faster, her eyes tried to close. And she waited—for the feel of his lips brushing hers, for the heat of his body resting against hers. She arched her back, leaned toward him. Held her breath as she felt desire bloom deep inside her.

And that reaction, that sudden craving for his touch, jolted her to reality the way nothing else could. With a strangled gasp, she scrambled backward until her spine rested against his car door. She didn't want this, would never want this. Not with Logan—not after everything that had passed between them. She would do well to remember that. The past was dead and she was never, *never* going back there again.

"You're right." The words emerged stilted and abrupt, but she was proud of herself for squeezing sound through her suddenly tight throat. "You're right. We're not going to agree on the past—our versions of what happened are too different. But we don't have to. All we have to do is work together to make sure that Luke is happy and well-adjusted."

Logan didn't answer right away. Instead, he looked out at the dark ocean as it crashed against the rocks. Were they destined to end up like that? Forever crash-

ing against each other until one of them completely
eroded the other?

She hoped not—she didn't want to disappear any
more than she wanted Logan to.

"So, what do you suggest?" he finally asked, his
voice as husky as hers.

"What's wrong with taking it slow?" He started
to interrupt, but she held up a hand. "I'm not saying
you need to wait until next week to see Luke, but let's
take this thing day by day. See how it goes."

"I'm not going to change my mind, Paige."

"Maybe not," she acknowledged in what she figured was a big concession for her. "But that doesn't
mean Luke won't get overwhelmed if you're always
in his face. You've been absent until now. Too much,
too soon might upset him."

"Maybe you're right. I don't want to push too hard
and you know him better than I do, obviously. I can
let you set the limits for him for now."

Not exactly thrilled with the *for now* part of his
comment, but happy that they were at least making
progress, Paige bit her tongue to hold back the sar-
castic comment that was right there, waiting to come
out. Logan was trying to see her side of the argument,
to acknowledge that his wasn't the only position, and
that had to be good enough for her. *For now.*

"Thank you for that," she said with a small smile.
"So, why don't we meet somewhere in the middle on

this? We can start with lunch at Prospector's tomorrow, see how that goes. If it works out, maybe you can take him to a movie this weekend. There are a couple out right now that he's dying to see."

"That sounds really good, actually." He seemed surprised, and she wondered, again, if she'd been too vehement in her protection of Luke. She had a hard time understanding that not every change in their lives was a threat to Luke.

"All right then." She nodded, blew out a breath. "So we'll see you tomorrow. Does twelve-thirty sound okay?"

It did, and as she watched him drive away a couple of minutes later, Paige was aware that she was heading down a path from which there was no return. All she could do now was hope that both she and her son made it to the finish line unscathed.

## CHAPTER NINE

"DON'T WORRY SO MUCH," Penny said to Paige five days later as she coated her roller in yellow paint. The electricians and drywall guys had finished in the bedroom this morning and the two of them were attacking the walls with gusto. "I'm sure they're doing fine together."

"I know you're right," Paige answered, glancing out the window for what had to be the fifteenth time in as many minutes. There was still no red truck pulling into the driveway, still no sign of her son and his father. It wasn't that she was worried. It was just that— "They were due back from the movie at six o'clock."

"And it's not even six-thirty. Maybe they stopped for a hamburger or something."

Paige nodded, because she'd already thought of that. In the days since Logan and Luke had officially met, the two had become thick as thieves and Luke was always conspiring for a way to spend more time with his dad.

After their lunch date at Prospector's last

Wednesday, the three of them had gone to the park, where she had sat on the grass and watched as Luke and Logan threw a football around. She'd enjoyed the afternoon quite a bit—and only part of that enjoyment had stemmed from the fact that she wasn't the one having to catch the ball.

Since then, they'd met at the beach once, where Luke and Logan had had a great time combing the sand for shells, hermit crabs and other sea life. Logan's ease and patience with their son was why she'd decided to okay the solo movie adventure this afternoon.

She'd thought it would be good for them to spend some time together without her. Being around Logan so much lately, seeing how he was with Luke, kept reminding her of all the things she had once loved about him. His patience. His intelligence. The innate sense of kindness that had him pausing from his own activities to talk to lonely old ladies or help someone look for a lost puppy. And since she couldn't afford to go there she'd figured a movie would be a low-key way for them to do that. After all, conversation wasn't required while a superhero was going head to head with his archnemesis.

But the movie had let out at 5:30 p.m. and they still weren't home. It was ridiculous to worry, but a part of her felt physically ill. What if there had been an accident? What if Logan had upset Luke and he'd

run away from him? What if Logan had grabbed their
son and fled the jurisdiction? Sure, it was a crazy
idea, but crazier things had been known to happen.

"I wish I'd gone with them," she said as she painted
her side of room.

"You can't be with them all the time, you know.
Besides, if you went with them, who'd help me finish
this room? The furniture you ordered is coming on
Wednesday."

Paige let her sister distract her, as she knew Penny
was trying to do. "I know. I can't wait to see the bed
in here. It's going to be gorgeous with these wood
floors, and that area rug I picked up the other day."

"I can't believe how good you are at this sort of
thing," Penny said. "I could study catalogs for weeks
and still not come up with the perfect combination the
way you do. These rooms are going to be gorgeous
when they're done."

"It's practice, no big deal."

"It's a huge deal. You left here with nothing and
put yourself through school as well as taking care of
a baby and work."

"You make me sound like an after-school
special."

"No. I make you sound like an inspiration, which
is why you're uncomfortable. You can't stand it when
anyone notices how awesome you are."

Paige laughed, pretended to buff her fingernails on her shirt. "What can I say? Some people have it—"

"And some people don't!" chimed in Penny. "And it doesn't even count as bragging if it's true."

"Sure it does. But since only my sister is around to hear me—"

"Only your sister? I'm hurt." Paige pouted.

Paige coated her roller with paint before moving along the wall. "No, you're not. You're pretending to be so I'll feel bad."

"Maybe a little. But only because—"

"It keeps my mind off the fact that Luke is now over half an hour late."

"Exactly." Penny paused as if gathering her courage. "You know, Paige, I'm no fan of Logan's. I mean, what he did to you can't exactly be taken back with a few playdates—"

"I don't care about what he did to me anymore. That was over a long time ago. I care that he turned his back on Luke without so much as a backward glance. That's what he can't take back."

"I know. I agree. But at the same time, he's making Luke incredibly happy. That has to count for something, doesn't it?"

"I know, and it does. Why do you think I decided not to fight this thing? My only concern is what's going to happen when Luke gets to be old hat? When he isn't a novelty and it isn't as exciting to have a son around anymore."

"Who says Logan is going to get bored? Luke's not exactly a football position, you know. You've been around him for eight years, and from what I can tell, you've never been bored."

"Yeah, but—" Paige thought over what her sister was saying, and what she wasn't. "Are you trying to tell me I need to prepare myself, for Logan wanting to be in Luke's life long-term?"

Penny shrugged. "It's not like I'm exactly a fount of information on men. I mean, if I had a clue, I wouldn't have bought this rundown old place with a guy who was clearly, in retrospect, not committed to it or to me."

The bitterness in Penny's voice instigated a whole new set of worries in Paige. What would she do if Logan didn't bail at the end of the summer, or before? How was she supposed to deal with this whole father-son thing long term? Luke was her son, her baby, and she wasn't sure how cool she was with sharing him for the rest of his life—particularly with the man she wasn't ready to forgive for abandoning him in the first place.

"Do you really regret it, Penny? Sinking your money into this place?"

Her sister snorted. "What's not to regret? It's a behemoth with bad plumbing and even worse electrical. Not to mention the fact that it's an eyesore."

"You know you don't have to stay here, don't you?" Paige paused in rolling—and eyeing the driveway— to look straight into her sister's eyes. "Not in this house and not in this town. We could do the cosmetics on this place, flip it and you could take the money and go anywhere you want to in the world."

"Mmm, that sounds nice. I hear Greece is great this time of year."

"Do you want to go to Greece?"

"No, silly. I don't. I mean, I do, but not at the expense of selling this place." Penny glanced around the room. "I complain about it a lot, but I have to admit, it's growing on me. Besides, I'm not like you. I couldn't take off and wander the globe until I found a place to fit in."

"You wouldn't have to wander the globe. You could come to L.A. You know Luke and I would love to have you move in with us."

"And do what?"

"And be an accountant in L.A. That's what you're trained for and God knows, I could use a good CPA."

"I'll tell you what. You send me your stuff and I'll be *your* CPA. But I think I'm going to stay here."

"Why? What's so special about this town?"

Penny bit her lip, and this time it was she who

looked out the window. "Mom and Dad are here. I know you hate them—and you have every right to. The way they treated you growing up was—" She shook her head. "It was bad. But they were always good parents to me and now that Dad's getting older and is needing help around the house more often, I don't feel comfortable leaving."

Paige hated the resentment that rose at her sister's words, the pain that told her that her relationship with her parents was yet another bit of unfinished business. She should be glad that Penny was on good terms with their mom and dad, especially since it meant Paige didn't have to worry about stepping in to help out.

But her dad was pushing seventy, though her mom was younger, and logically she knew the time to reconcile was limited. This summer might be her best opportunity to change the dynamic with her parents… or to let the relationship languish as it had. It was her call, but she wasn't sure what she wanted. It was stupid to long for an emotional closeness she'd never had, but then again, wasn't that what she'd found herself suddenly doing with Logan as well? Trying to rewrite history when she should be focusing on the here and now?

Nice to know age and responsibility weren't enough to stop her from being a complete idiot. Not wanting to deal with her masochistic tendencies, she resumed painting, concentrating on rolling the yellow gloss over the walls as though it was the most important task she'd ever done.

As the minutes passed, she knew she needed to say something, knew that Penny was waiting anxiously for her to respond. But what to say? Most of the words that crawled through her were ugly, and, if she voiced them, would put Penny in an untenable position.

Or maybe not so untenable, she realized with dawning horror. Maybe Penny would tell her to get out. Would choose her parents the way everyone always had and leave Paige out in the cold.

She didn't want that to happen, couldn't let that happen. For the first time in recent memory, she craved the closeness and connection of family. Maybe it was too many years standing on her own. Maybe it was confronting Logan and this town and the ensuing changes to her life. Or maybe it didn't matter why. It was sufficient to acknowledge she wanted— needed—her sister. So Paige had to suck things up. Again. Keep her mouth shut when what she really wanted to do was ask what it was about her that was so damn unlovable that no one ever chose her. No one ever stayed with her. Even Luke was drifting away, spellbound by his newfound father.

Her breathing sawed in and out, a little harsher than before.

"Paige? Are you okay?"

She tried to speak around the lump that had taken up residence there yet couldn't. She cleared her throat. "I'm fine. Just worried about Luke."

"Paige, I didn't mean to upset—"

"I'm not upset. At least not with you. But if Logan doesn't get my kid here soon, I'm going to lose my mind."

There was a long silence, and Paige knew her sister was deciding whether or not to believe her. "Why don't you call him?"

"I should. But I was trying to be good, trying to show him that I trust him with Luke."

"Even though you don't."

"Exactly. But doubt and suspicion don't exactly foster a decent relationship, so I'm trying, right?"

Penny shook her head. "You know you're warped, don't you?"

She meant it as a joke—or at least Paige thought she did—but that didn't keep the words from hitting a little close to home. She felt like a freak here in Prospect, Oregon. Had always felt like one.

From the time she was young and realized that the way her parents treated her was very different than how they treated Penny, she'd known something was wrong with her. The way people whispered behind their hands when her mom took the two of them into town. The way she would catch her mother looking at

her sometimes, as if she wanted to cry just because
Paige existed.

It wasn't exactly an idyllic way to grow up. And
if it left her with trust issues, even after all this time,
then she figured she was entitled to them.

It wasn't until years later, when Penny was peek-
ing at their mother's diary—Paige would never have
dared for fear of serious retaliation—that the two of
them pieced together what had made Paige different.
She was the daughter of an affair her mother had had
while her father was serving overseas in the army.
Her parents hated her because she was a tangible
reminder of her mother's infidelity, her brief relationship with a man who wasn't her husband.

That was the day Paige had realized that no matter
how good she was, no matter how many awards she
won or how many A's she brought home, she would
never be good enough for her parents. And from that
moment forward, her life had gone into a downward
spiral that hadn't ended until she was working as a
waitress in L.A., going to night school and waiting
for Luke to be born.

Her life had turned out all right—better than all
right, thanks to her neighbor, Lucas, and his connec-
tions in the film industry—so maybe it was selfish of
Paige to resent Penny's good relationship with their
parents. But she couldn't help it.

She didn't wish the same kind of childhood she

had on Penny—she wouldn't wish the verbal, emotional and sometimes physical abuse on anyone—but she did resent that her sister had seen it and still managed to maintain a relationship with their parents. Almost as if it was okay for them to hurt Paige, as long as they didn't hurt Penny as well.

Hating the way she was feeling, Paige tried to shove all the negative emotions deep down inside, where she wouldn't be forced to examine them anymore. It was hard, but she refused to waste her time being bitter over things she couldn't change. It wasn't as though she needed their approval to be happy.

"So, which bedroom are we painting next?" she asked Penny, determined not to drown in her own self-pity party.

Her sister latched on to the question like the conversational lifeboat it was. "I think we should do the blue room. The electricians finished in there yesterday, and I want to start pulling up the tile in the bathroom. If we can get the room painted, they can get in there and refinish the floor and we'll actually have two fully complete guest rooms."

"Minus furniture."

"Well, yes, but I'll take care of that when I'm in Portland tomorrow."

"Woo-hoo. We are definitely making progress."

Paige bent to load her roller with more paint, and as she did, she glanced outside for what had to be the three thousandth time. This time, however, Logan's truck was making the trek up the long and winding road to the house.

"Luke's home," she said as she laid down her roller and headed for the door at close to a run.

With an effort, she unclenched her jaw, plastered a smile on her face that she was far from feeling. Just because she was out of sorts and annoyed didn't mean that Luke had to be—or even that he had to know about it. She'd found one of the good things about children was that they were entirely self-absorbed most of the time. Hopefully he'd be too busy telling her about all the cool parts in the movie to wonder why she was a little off.

By the time she got her hands washed and got downstairs, Luke and Logan were hanging out on the porch. The door was open and it was obvious that Luke had invited his father in. It was just as obvious that Logan had declined the invitation. She didn't know if it was because he was in a hurry to leave or because she had yet to invite him into her sister's house. Judging from the way he was lounging on the porch swing, she had a feeling it was the latter— and appreciated his restraint. She wasn't sure she was ready to let him in any farther than the porch— literally or figuratively.

"So, how was the movie?" she asked as she walked outside, making sure to close the door behind her.

"It was great, Mom. Fabulous. The hero was su-percool. He had all kinds of awesome powers, like he could get inside the bad guy's mind and make him…" Luke filled her in about the movie, including its twists and turns and not-so-surprise ending.

When he finally wound down, Logan laughed and said, "I hope you weren't planning on going to see it anytime soon."

"Why would I, when I received such a wonderful plot summary right here?" She bent and brushed her lips over Luke's soft, black curls. "Thanks, baby. You made me feel like I was right there in that theater with you."

"That would have been cool. Dad let me get pop-corn and candy and an Icee. It was awesome. And then we went to get a hamburger afterward. Because all those stunts really worked up my appetite."

She raised her eyebrows. "Really? You had an ap-petite after popcorn, candy and an Icee? Those must have been some stunts."

Sensing danger, or at least the beginnings of a lecture on nutrition, she could almost see the wheels turning in her son's head as he tried to figure out the best way to duck out on her. "They were. In fact, I think I'm kind of tired. I'm gonna go up to my room and rest for a while." He turned to Logan. "Thanks, Dad. I had a lot of fun." He wrapped his arms tightly around Logan's waist and squeezed for all he was worth before scampering through the front door at close to a run.

Paige watched him go, a little surprised at the depths of emotion displayed in that hug. Seemed he was as susceptible to Logan's charm as his mother always had been. Her heart hurt at the thought, enough so that she smiled at Logan for his part in making her child happy instead of laying into him for worrying her.

"Well, you're certainly a big hit today," she said lightly.

"I guess." Logan shoved an uncomfortable hand through his hair. "I'm really sorry about being late. At first, I thought it'd only take about fifteen minutes to stop for burgers, but—"

"But Luke turned it into a three-ring circus?"

"Exactly. It took him almost ten minutes to order, and then he didn't want to eat half as much as he wanted to play on the playset or mess with the toy that came with his meal."

"And then, when you were ready to leave, he decided to suddenly get interested in his dinner, right?"

"Yeah!"

"Believe me, I know the drill. It's a pretty common occurrence at our house."

"I bet. Still, I should have called. It won't happen again."

She nodded. "Thanks for that."

"He's a great kid, Paige. I know I've said this before, but I'm so impressed with what you've done with him, all on your own."

She felt herself flush with pleasure. "He is pretty wonderful, isn't he?"

"Absolutely. And he talked about you constantly—everything was 'Mom would like this, I wonder if Mom knows, Mom told me…'" He shrugged sheepishly. "It's obvious that he thinks you're the greatest thing since sliced bread."

"Yeah, well, the feeling is entirely mutual." She paused for a second, part of her wanting nothing more than to kick this guy to the curb. But she was smart enough to figure out that was her fear talking, because another, bigger part of her really wanted him to stick around for a while.

"So, do you want to hang out for a few minutes? Maybe have a glass of lemonade? I'm pretty much done with my half of the slave labor for the day."

He glanced at his watch. "Normally I would be all over that. But I'm working tonight. I had to trade parole with one of my men in order to get tomorrow off for the carnival."

She was glad that he had remembered something that Luke was so completely looking forward to, but it didn't surprise her. When they'd been together, Logan had always remembered little things that made her happy, things that no one else would ever have paid attention to.

Despite her worries for her son, Paige felt her guard lower a little bit. She didn't know many men would have made such an effort to be a part of their son's life at this late date. It would have been easier for him to write Luke off, especially since Logan probably still planned to start a family some day. An eight-year-old kid with the town tramp had a tendency to mess with plans like that—particularly in a place like Prospect.

Maybe he had changed after all. It was a disconcerting thought, considering what it meant for Luke's future—and her own. If Logan was really in this for the long haul, then she had to prepare herself for some major changes.

Surprisingly, that thought unfurled a little bud of hope deep inside her. One she'd thought had disappeared long ago. She didn't know yet how she felt about that—the idea was even more frightening than the idea of having him in Luke's life for the duration.

But she could take a lot if it meant Luke finally got the father he obviously wanted and so richly deserved.

"So, what do you say, Paige? Do you want to go to the carnival with Luke and me? It might be fun if we all go together?"

"I was planning on it. Managing a kid at a busy carnival takes some practice."

"Right, of course." He smiled. "Good. I was really hoping you'd come, not necessarily to manage Luke but that's as good a reason as any if it means you'll be our date."

She wasn't quite sure how to respond to that, or the way he was looking at her—as if he'd been able to read her thoughts earlier. And had agreed on them. That made her nervous, had her tripping over her tongue when she said, "I'm looking forward to going. It's been a long time since I went to a carnival at the Prospect Fairgrounds."

But as soon as the words were out, Paige wished she could recall them. Logan's eyes had darkened to a gunmetal gray and she could see awareness in them. Could see the memory of that long-ago trip to the fairgrounds.

They'd only been dating for a little while when he'd taken her to the annual fair, and they'd barely been able to keep their hands off each other long enough for Logan to pay for their tickets. Once they'd gained admittance, Logan had dragged her through the entire carnival to the funhouse, refusing to stop to talk to any of his friends who called out to them.

Once they'd gotten to the attraction, he'd bought the requisite number of ride tickets, then had tossed them at the operator in his haste to get her inside, where they'd spent well over an hour making out in the dark corners of the shadowy structure.

The air between them now turned electric. With each breath she took, Paige felt as though she was drawing sparks into her lungs, little, shimmery shocks of electricity that skated along her nerve endings until her nipples ached and her core throbbed.

She wasn't sure how much of the attraction was based on the memory and how much of it was because of the strong, handsome, virile man standing in front of her. The one who had taken such good care of her son.

For a minute they were in high school, before any bad stuff had happened. They'd been crazy about each other, and though she knew the past would never be the future, for one minute, she didn't care. For one minute, all she wanted was to feel what it was like to be held by Logan, kissed by Logan, loved by Logan. None of the guys she'd ever been with had ever played her body half so well as he had, had paid attention to her every breath and whimper the way he had.

She wanted nothing more than to fling herself at him, to beg him to kiss her. To plead with him to make her feel the way he once had. It had been so long since a man had touched her, so long since she'd let someone close to her, that the temptation to feel again—with him—was nearly overwhelming.

The heat in his eyes convinced her that Logan

was feeling the same way, a fact that both scared and delighted her. She told herself to say good-night, told herself to retreat. This was dangerous ground. But she did neither. Remained there, pinned by the power and the passion in his molten silver eyes.

"Paige." His voice was so low and rough she had to strain to understand each syllable he spoke. "Tell me to go."

She swallowed, tried to speak, but her mouth was desert dry. She cleared her throat, tried again to no avail. Licked her lips, then gasped as she realized he was watching her tongue trace her bottom lip with the intense, focused concentration of a wild bird of prey.

Her heartbeat was a crazy, mixed-up symphony inside her.

Her breath came in a series of harsh, broken waves she could no longer control.

And her body, her crazy, desperate, out-of-control body was shaking like a junkie desperate for a fix.

The sensations were nothing new—Logan had always inspired this reaction in her—but it had been so long and things were so messed up between them that she didn't know what to do.

Didn't know how to react.

Didn't know if she should stay or if she should run inside, bolting the door behind her.

In the end, she didn't have to do anything, because

Logan came for her. He stepped forward until his body was only inches from hers. So close that she could feel the heat radiating from him in waves and could smell the sweet, lemony scent of his breath.

She knew it was stupid to stand like this with him, knew it was insane to even think about opening herself up to Logan again. Yet there was something about him—had always been something about him—that drew her like a moth to a flame. No matter how determined she was that she wouldn't get burned this time around, she found herself pulled in despite herself.

"Logan." It was a whimper, a plea, though she didn't have a clue what she was asking for.

"Paige."

"I need—"

"I know, darlin'."

"How?" Her breath broke.

"Because I need it, too."

He cupped her cheek, his thumb stroking gently over her lips—once, twice—before he slid his hand to the back of her head. His fingers tangled in her hair, tugged a little, and she felt an answering heat streak through her body. And then he was inching her forward, bending his head as he lowered his mouth gently to hers.

Paige gasped as his lips brushed her own, soft as a butterfly's wings. She wasn't sure what she expected from him—maybe the impatience of his youth—but this sweet restraint wasn't it. And yet it caught her, made her crave the taste of him until she could think of nothing, of no one, but him.

Her hands slid up his chest, vaguely cataloguing the hard muscles there before she slipped them into the shaggy hair at the base of his neck and tried to tug him closer. Tried to get a proper kiss from him.

If this was the only moment she would have with him, then she would take it. She would grab it with both hands and say to hell with the consequences—at least for a little while. At least for the duration of this one, perfect kiss.

## CHAPTER TEN

WHAT THE HELL WAS HE DOING? Logan wondered wildly, even as he pulled Paige's body flush against his own. He knew he should stop, knew he should walk to his truck before things got out of control. Even as the thought came to him, he knew he wasn't going to do it. He couldn't. Separating himself from Paige now, before he got a taste of her sexy mouth, was unthinkable.

He told himself he hadn't wanted this to happen, hadn't planned for it when he invited her to go the carnival with him and Luke. But he knew the truth. It wasn't only the look on her face—the proof that she remembered the last time they had gone to the fairgrounds together as clearly as he did—that had undone him. It was being around her this past week. Seeing her smile. Hearing her tease Luke. Smelling her sweet, crazy scent.

At odd moments at the park and on the beach, he'd found himself transfixed by her and the way she threw herself into whatever she was doing—whether it was playing football with Luke or playing tag with the waves.

Paige had always been like that, once he'd gotten past the hard outer shell she presented to the world. Had always been so full of life and excitement that she made him feel the same way. When they'd been young, all he'd needed to get aroused was hear her laugh. He wasn't sure how he felt about the fact that time hadn't changed that.

He did know that he wasn't going to let the past stop him from kissing her now. As he brushed his mouth over hers one more time, asking for entrance— for acceptance—Paige parted her lips on a soft moan. It was a low, breathy sound that shot through him, ratcheting up his arousal to flashpoint and taking him from gentle to demanding in the space between one thought and the next.

All the blood in his body rushed south, and his erection throbbed, until all he could think of was getting closer to her. Getting inside her as quickly as possible. And since there was no way for him to get inside her lush body, he would make do with a kiss.

Crushing his mouth against hers, Logan slid his tongue along the fullness of her bottom lip. She whimpered, her hands tugging at his hair and it was all he could do to keep from shoving her against the wall and taking her here on the front porch with their son and her sister inside the house.

Because he couldn't do what he wanted, what he needed, he contented himself with exploring her mouth with his tongue, taking her, tasting her. She was everything he remembered—dark, warm honey and soft, ripe apricots—and more. So much more. Wild like the ocean that was beyond reach. Sweet like the summer strawberries he could eat by the bucketful.

Her taste got to him, wound itself around him, became a part of him. Made him crazy and burned him alive. All he could feel or hear or see or taste was her. Pulling her head back for better access, he deepened the kiss. Ran his tongue over the roof of her mouth and along the sensitive inner seams of her lips. Tangled it with hers, before pulling back and nipping at her lower lip.

She gasped again, her arms twining around his neck as she melted into him, the incredible softness of her body making him desperate with the need to be inside her one more time.

When he'd been a teenager, being inside Paige had been the most pleasure he'd ever felt, but as he'd grown older he'd convinced himself that he'd imagined the connection. That he'd remembered it wrong. That the passion and need that had woken him up in the middle of the night for years after she'd left were figments of his imagination. It wasn't possible for him to have felt everything that he dreamed, everything that he fantasized about.

But he'd been wrong. It wasn't that he remembered too much, it was that he hadn't remembered enough. Those sweaty, sexy dreams couldn't compare to the reality of having her in his arms again, her body trembling against his as she opened herself to him. As she let him take her, let him ravage her, in an effort to soothe the savage emotions ripping through him at an alarming rate.

It didn't work. Nothing did. Need was a Molotov cocktail inside him, and he ground his mouth against hers in an effort to absorb everything she had to give. Sucked her lower lip between his teeth and bit her in an effort to absorb her very essence.

She whimpered and he tried to stop, afraid that he had hurt her with the crazy mix of emotions rushing through him. But she wouldn't let him go, her hands clutching his shoulders, twisting in the soft fabric of his shirt in a desperate attempt to keep him with her.

It was all the encouragement he needed, and Logan lost himself in her softness, in her desire. He kissed her and kissed her and kissed her, until his lips felt swollen and tingling against hers and his body screamed for relief. And still she held on to him, as if all the years and pain and betrayal between them no longer mattered.

In the end, all those things did matter—more now than they ever had. And he wasn't a teenager who couldn't control himself, who would rather have sex now and worry about the consequences later. He had a son—*they* had a son—and the relationship between the three of them was so precarious that he didn't want to do anything to threaten it, no matter how good it felt to hold her in his arms again.

With that thought uppermost in his mind, he forced himself to pull back slowly, his lips pressing gentle kisses to the corners of her mouth, to her chin, to the little dimple that had driven him insane for most of junior high and all of high school.

Then he let her go, because no matter how much he wished differently, they weren't kids anymore. They couldn't do things simply because they felt good.

He brushed her bangs off her cheek, kissed her forehead and watched as Paige came slowly back to herself. For long seconds, those beautiful green eyes of hers blazed like the most fiery of emeralds before slowly dimming, darkening.

She stepped back, shoved her hands in the pockets of her jeans. "Wow."

"That's what I was thinking."

"I don't—I'm sorry—I— Where did that come from?"

He grinned despite the layers of complication he had added to their relationship. "My guess is from where it always came from, darlin'. It isn't like we weren't compatible in that area before."

Her cheeks flushed a soft, becoming apricot and he was reminded, again, of how good she tasted. His hands ached with the need to touch her, to pull her against him, but he clenched them into fists and ignored the strange and unexpected pain that came with separating himself from her.

"I should probably…" She gestured to the door behind her.

"Absolutely. I need to go anyway. I'm supposed to be at the station in—" he checked his watch "—ten minutes."

"You're going to be late."

"I am."

Neither of them made a move to leave.

"Thanks again for taking Luke to the movies."

He shook his head. "I already told you, I enjoyed it."

"Right." She still didn't turn to go inside.

"Is it okay if I pick you guys up at five o'clock for the carnival?"

"That sounds good." She smiled at him and Logan felt his control slip another notch or three. He almost reached for her, probably would have if his cell phone hadn't picked that moment to issue the special ring he'd programmed for the station.

"I really have to go," he said, reaching for his phone as he backed away.

"Okay. Have a good night, Logan."

"You, too, Paige."

He rushed down the stairs, answering the phone as he went. Sure enough, it was a call from Lisa at the station, and as usual the news she had to deliver wasn't good. They'd gotten another call about raised voices over at the Finley place.

Shaking his head as he threw his truck into gear and headed over there—he didn't need an address as it was the third such call he'd received in the past couple of months—he swore that this time he was hauling Graham Finley into jail, whether his wife wanted to press charges or not. That man needed a wake-up call and fast—there was no way Logan was going to let him beat up his wife any longer. Not on his watch and not in his jurisdiction.

Sure enough, when he pulled up in front of the old house on the outskirts of town, every light in the place was on. The ambulance Lisa had called had obviously made it a few minutes before him, as the paramedics were already at the door, talking to a very distraught—and very bruised—Barbara Finley.

From where he was sitting, it didn't appear as if

she was cooperating, but then, that wasn't exactly a surprise. No matter what he told her, no matter what promises he made that he would keep her safe, she absolutely refused to testify against her husband.

And while state law said he could arrest the bastard—and even prosecute him if the district attorney agreed—without her testimony, he had no real proof. Not when she insisted that she'd walked into a door or fell down the steps.

But just because he might not be able to make a case against Finley in a court of law, didn't mean he wasn't going to pull the man out of here tonight. Let him cool his jets in jail for a few days—the judge was on vacation and wouldn't be back for four days. No judge meant no arraignment and no bail, which meant Finley wouldn't be beating on his wife for a little while anyway.

It was a shitty solution, but it was better than leaving the man here. And maybe, if he got her away from her abusive husband for longer than a few hours, he'd have a shot at convincing Barbara that she had other, better options than sticking around and waiting for him to kill her.

Already tense and more than a little bit wary, Logan approached the front door, where two paramedics and one of his deputies stood talking to Barbara. Through the dining-room window that overlooked the street, he could see Graham sitting at the table, eating his dinner. It took a cool son-of-a-bitch, and one who was damned sure of his wife, to keep eating his pot roast while his wife, whom he had beat the hell out of, stood at the door talking to the police.

Anger crawled up Logan's spine. But he forced himself to stay ice cold and unfeeling. He could be pissed all he wanted later. Right now, he had a job to do.

"Hello, Barbara," he said to the woman who had been his date to the seventh grade Sadie Hawkins dance.

"Oh, hi, Logan. I'm glad you're here. Will you please tell these men that I don't need any assistance?" Her voice was impatient, but she wouldn't look him in the eye. "I'm perfectly fine."

Logan looked her over from head to toe, cataloguing the damage as he went. A black eye, an uneven jaw that he would bet was broken, bruises up and down her arms, including the one she was cradling to her body as if it was too sore to leave by her side. Her wrist was already swollen and a quick glance at Cal, the paramedic in charge of the scene, told him that the man was pretty sure it was broken.

"I've got to be honest with you, Barb. You look pretty banged up. I think a trip to the hospital is going to be a necessity here."

"Don't be silly. I tripped and hit my head on

the kitchen counter." Her voice broke. "It's no big deal."

He gritted his teeth, wished not for the first time that he had a female officer on his squad. He'd gone through all the sensitivity training for domestic disputes in Seattle, made sure his officers here did the same thing, but that didn't mean he was an expert on how to talk to battered women.

"Maybe we could come in and talk to you about your fall. The neighbors who called 911 said there was some loud yelling coming from over here."

"Graham and I were having an argument," she agreed. "That's how I tripped—I wasn't paying attention."

Logan forced himself not to react to her blatant lies, then spent the next few minutes going round and round with Barbara, trying to get her to admit the truth. She refused to, but when he finally talked his way into the house, he found Graham with skinned knuckles on both of his large hands, as well as some blood on his arm that didn't appear to have come from him.

It was enough to make an arrest, especially with the statements from two of the neighbors who'd heard and seen most of the fight. Barbara was upset, and she pleaded with Logan to let her husband go. Told him he was making a huge mistake.

He refused to let her pleas sway him as he read

Graham his rights, hoping that once he hauled her husband away in cuffs, Cal and his partner could convince Barbara to go to the hospital, but he wasn't holding his breath. Especially as she followed him all the way to the car, begging him not to take her husband in.

Reaching into the glove compartment of his truck, he pulled out a card for Sarah Jerome—a psychologist in town who provided counseling to abused women. She even ran a small shelter out of her clinic, and as he handed the card to Barbara, Logan said, "You don't have to stay here. I know we've talked about this before, but you need to let me help you, Barbara. I can take you to the hospital, get you fixed up and we can take you to Sarah. She'd take you in, help you build a new life for yourself."

He glanced at the house. "You can't stay here. He's getting worse."

"He's my husband." Her chin trembled as she spoke, as if every word she said was an agony.

"He's going to kill you one day and you know it. So why are you staying?"

"He'll kill me if I leave."

"I won't let him, Barbara. I promise you. I'll protect you. The department will keep you safe."

"For how long?" She shook her head. "No, I'll take my chances here with Graham. But thanks for asking, Logan. It means a lot."

"At least let me take you to the hospital, then."

"Logan—"

"For old times' sake. I'll even stay with you for a while, if you want me to."

It seemed she was on the brink of accepting. Then she shook her head regretfully and slowly walked to the house. Her head was bowed and every step she took was obviously painful. But she never looked back and he had to force himself not to punch the nearest wall—or Graham Finley's face.

By the time he was done processing Graham, and writing up the paperwork—which included several very unique threats issued by Graham toward him, it was close to midnight and his mood had gone from bad to worse.

Normally midnight rolling around was a good thing, as 12:00 to 6:00 a.m. was Prospect's slow time—unlike Seattle, when the perps were just getting started. But the tourists had started arriving in the previous weekend, which meant he was probably going to spend the rest of his night dealing with underage drinking and drunk and disorderlies.

It turned out he was right, and by the time he finally made it home to bed, he was pissed off and tired as hell. Not to mention more sexually frustrated than he could remember being in a long time. At first he'd planned on heading straight to bed but by the time he stripped off his clothes, he knew there was no way he was going to get to sleep, at least not without a cold shower first.

As he stood under the frigid water, he couldn't help thinking about what Paige's mouth had felt like under his, couldn't help reliving those moments when her body had been pressed so tightly to his. He'd wanted to pull her tank top over her head, to lower his mouth to her breasts and roll her nipples over his tongue, between his teeth. Had wanted to rip her jeans off and put his mouth all over her, licking and tasting every inch of her glorious body.

He'd wanted to know if it felt the same—if she felt the same—as it had nearly a decade ago. Kissing her had felt the same—but different as well. It was as exciting as ever, but she was more dominant now. More sure of herself, as if she'd changed everything about herself during her time in L.A.

He had to admit, much as he might wish otherwise, Los Angeles seemed to agree with her—and Luke. He'd never forget the first time he'd been sitting in a theater in Seattle, watching the credits—his ex-wife had a thing about credits—and seen Paige's name scroll across the screen. At first he hadn't believed it was the same Paige he'd grown up with, but ten minutes on Google had convinced him otherwise. Despite all the odds, Paige had landed on her feet. Hell, she'd even been nominated for an Oscar for her work on a big-budget movie two years ago.

It had been a hell of a kick in the pants, though not as big a kick as realizing he had a son was—or that he was still attracted to his son's mother, even after everything that had gone between them.

He didn't want to want Paige, didn't want to want anything to do with her outside of Luke. It complicated an already difficult situation. But today, on that porch, something had clicked between them—that same thing that had always been there. A whole lot of sexual attraction underscored by something else, something he'd once called love but now knew was merely a heavy-duty case of lust.

It wasn't as though he was still in love with her after all this time. How could he be? He'd moved on, had rarely given her a thought the past few years. Hell, he'd even been married. Surely those weren't the actions of a man who was still carrying a torch for his high-school sweetheart.

Besides, he couldn't forget that she hadn't tried to contact him in years.

Maybe he could get past the fact that she'd cheated on him when he would have died for her—she'd had a rough time of things and he could understand how being happy might have scared her—but he'd never be able to understand why she hadn't picked up the phone to tell him about Luke.

Yes, he'd hung up on her sister when she'd called and that would forever be his guilt to carry. But at the same time, Paige could have tried again. On Luke's first birthday or his second. She could have phoned him or sent him a picture, something to let him know that he was a father. That he had a son who needed him. He wanted that time with his son back, needed that time back.

But that wasn't going to happen. He couldn't change the past, any more than he could convince Barbara Finley to leave Graham.

His bad mood a million times worse, Logan slammed the shower off, then grabbed a towel before heading into his bedroom. So much for a cold shower—he was more frustrated now, mentally and physically, than he had been before he'd tried the time-honored remedy. As he climbed into bed and flipped out the light, he had a feeling sleep was still far off.

"WANT A SPOON?" PENNY ASKED, holding up a tube of chocolate chip cookie dough. "I just opened it."

"You're not supposed to eat that stuff raw, you know. There have been salmonella scares."

"I like to live on the edge. Danger is my middle name."

Paige raised an eyebrow at her sister, who was currently decked out in hot pink pajamas sporting white poodles on perfume bottles. "I can see that.

The bunny slippers are a particularly frightening touch."

"Bite me."

"Careful. I might take you up on that. God knows, there's not enough cookie dough in the world to make me feel better tonight."

"Who rained on your parade, Little Miss Sunshine?"

Paige snorted. "Who do you think?"

"Well, sit down and tell me all about it. I've been told that I have a very soft shoulder to cry on."

"I can imagine. But you go first."

"Me? What makes you think I have any problems?"

"Besides the fact that you single-handedly ate an entire roll of cookie dough?"

"Not an *entire* roll. You can still scrape the sides."

"I think I'll pass, thanks." Paige grabbed a bag of chips before hopping onto the counter next to her sister. "So, spill."

"Just the same old thing. I was going through the expenses, preparing for my trip to Portland tomorrow, and there's never enough money. I mean, there would have been, if Mike had stuck around. We had everything planned out down to the last dollar." She shook her head. "But without his bank account, things are a lot tighter around here than I had imagined they would be."

"I already told you I'd be happy to help, Penny. Trying to do everything yourself is stupid."

"You are helping. You've laid tile and stained wood, painted walls and planted trees. And you've given me back my sister, which means more than all the rest put together. I don't need your money, too."

"Come on, Penny. I have plenty of the stuff. Being successful in Hollywood, even behind the scenes, pays pretty well, in case you didn't know."

"That doesn't make it right."

"You let me decide what's right. How much do you need?"

"Paige. I'm serious. I can't take your money."

"Why not?"

"Because. How long did you struggle on your own, working two jobs and trying to take care of a baby all by yourself?"

"What does that have to do with anything?"

"I had everything. I had parents who paid for me to go to college, a good job and I threw it all away on a guy. You—you did everything by yourself and yet here you are. You deserve everything you have and there's no way I'm going to be a part of taking any of that away."

"Do you think I wanted to do all these things on my own? I would have done anything to have you with me, if for no other reason than to give me a hug and tell me everything was going to be all right."

"Exactly. I've never done anything for you and you uprooted your whole life to come here this summer."

"And I'd do it again in a heartbeat. When we were kids, you did everything for me. You saved me when I couldn't figure out which way was up, stood between Dad and me when things got too crazy. What makes you think that I'm not being selfish in wanting to help you?"

"What do you mean?"

Paige thought quickly, tried to figure out a way to get her sister to take the money she was offering. She wasn't filthy rich or anything, but the last few movies had paid extremely well, especially once she moved up to head set designer. "What if we became partners?" she asked.

"What do you mean?"

"You were going to partner with Mike, right? So what if I take his place? Put in the same amount of money you do, and then we'll have equal ownership of the B and B. I'll be a silent partner and you'll have to do most of the work while I'm in L.A., which means you'll get a majority of the profits, and—"

"You would do that? You'd be my partner in the inn?"

"Why wouldn't I? You don't seem to understand

how much I miss you, Penny. How much I want you to be a big part of Luke's and my life."

"I want the same thing!" Penny squealed. "So we're really going to do this? We're going to become partners?"

"Absolutely. Luke's going to be thrilled."

Penny threw her arms around her and squeezed her so tightly Paige was afraid she'd crack a rib. But she hugged her sister as tightly and tried to ignore how with every day that passed, her life seemed to become more and more tied to Prospect. Being a silent partner in a business was no big deal, but being her sister's silent partner—that was something else all together.

She'd once sworn she'd never come back here and now it felt like she might never get away again. Penny and Logan were wrapping more invisible strings around her every day, until Paige could barely think with the need to escape. Not from them, but from the past she'd spent so long running from.

This week it had caught up to her with a vengeance. Too bad she didn't have a clue what to do about it.

## CHAPTER ELEVEN

LOGAN COULDN'T REMEMBER the last time he'd had this much fun, wasn't sure he ever had before—at least not in his adult life. After making sure Luke was fastened and that his back was flat against the wall of the ride, he strapped himself in as well. There was nothing like going to a hokey little carnival with his son to make him remember the joy and excitement of his childhood.

Once he was fastened, he glanced over the crowd below them, hoping to see Paige. When he couldn't find her, he felt a small flare of disappointment. It set off a whole series of alarm bells at the back of his consciousness, one that warned him that lust might not be the only thing he felt for his son's mother.

The thought made him ridiculously uncomfortable. He tried to shy away from it, from any thoughts of her, and might have accomplished it if Luke hadn't chosen that second to slip his fingers through the bars between them and grab his wrist.

"You okay, buddy?" he asked.

"Yeah. I just wanted to hold your hand. Mom always lets me hold hers until the ride gets started."

"Oh." Logan glanced at the little hand that was currently clutching his sleeve and felt something melt in the vicinity of his heart. "You bet you can hold my hand."

He bent his arm so that he could wrap his fingers around his son's. As those cold, dirty fingers curled around his own he thought this was what fatherhood was all about. Tiny moments such as these that he would remember for the rest of his life.

When the music started a few moments later, and the lights began flashing superbright, he wasn't sure if he was going to be able to release Luke's hand. It felt too good to touch him, too real—as though he was finally becoming the father he had always dreamed of being.

But Luke squirmed a little until Logan loosened his grip, and then they were off, spinning faster and faster, the centrifugal force keeping their backs pressed tightly against the walls of the ride.

Luke called out and Logan felt an instant of alarm. It took all of his strength to fight the centrifugal force, but he finally managed to turn his head to see his son laughing like a hyena. He found himself laughing as well, through the rest of the ride and beyond, while he was helping Luke get himself unfastened.

"That was so much fun, Dad! Let's do it again!"

"Sure. But why don't we do a few other rides first, then come back. I think I need a little break from high-speed circles."

"Let's do the rockets, then."

"Sounds like a plan."

Time passed in a blur as he followed Luke from ride to ride. A bunch of people saw them together and stopped to probe a little, all in the guise of friendly chitchat. He didn't make them work very hard before he introduced Luke as his son, and maybe that was a mistake, but it wasn't as though anyone looking at them could doubt their relationship.

Besides, people in Prospect had long memories and they all knew he had dated Paige before she'd left town nine years ago. The fact that her eight-year-old son was also his couldn't be that big a shock to anyone.

The past week had been the best of his adult life, and as he'd hung out with Luke he'd tried to let go of his anger at Paige, especially after their kiss. He wasn't planning to pick up where they'd left off— the intervening years made that impossible—but he wanted to get along with her, for all of their sakes. Wanted to see things from her point of view.

Yes, he'd been harsh when she'd told him about the baby. Yes, he had told her he never wanted to see her again. But damn it, he'd been hurting. He had been suspended from school for fighting his closest friend, who had claimed to have slept with Paige while Logan had been out of town looking at colleges. Mark had claimed that it was all her fault, that she had caught him drunk at a party and seduced him.

Logan hadn't believed him, had told him he was full of shit—that Paige loved him and wouldn't screw around on him. Mark had told him he was crazy, that they'd all understood why he'd gone slumming at the beginning, but that it was getting old, fast. Especially when she kept throwing herself at his friends behind his back.

He'd punched Mark and everything had escalated, until the two of them were rolling around on the locker room floor. The coaches broke it up, but not before Mark had screamed out a whole bunch of poison about Paige.

Logan had thought he hadn't believed it, had thought that he hadn't believed anything Mark or the others had said in the next few days. But his belief hadn't withstood a bunch of his good friends telling him the truth, or his mother admitting seeing Paige in town with other boys. He'd been shattered. Heartbroken and disgusted and humiliated.

When Paige had come over later that day, he had spewed his rage and embarrassment on her head. He could still see her face when she'd told him about the baby—pale and fragile and so nervous that a part of him had wanted nothing more than to pull her into his arms no matter how angry he was with her.

But he hadn't. Instead he'd heard her trying to pass off a baby on him that could belong to half the guys in school and he'd lost it. Told her to get the hell away from him. Told her she was a slut and that he never wanted to see her again.

She'd protested, had pleaded with him to believe her, but he'd hardened his heart against her and when she left, he'd felt a vicious sort of vindication that he had hurt her as much as she'd hurt him.

Now, years later, he was ashamed of that feeling, ashamed of what he'd done to her. He wasn't ashamed of breaking up with her—the idea of being with a woman who wasn't exclusively with him was still anathema to him. But he should have realized that condoms weren't a hundred percent effective, that though he'd always been careful, the odds that her baby had belonged to him were as high as they were for anyone else in town.

He'd blown her off and now he was paying the price. He'd spent eight years without his son, eight years missing out on all the amazing little details that made Luke the amazing kid that he was. And while part of him blamed Paige for not making him listen, for not serving him with paternity papers when Luke was born, he couldn't ignore his own culpability. As he'd stared at the ceiling last night, he'd forced himself to face the truth.

He'd made the decision to cut her out of his life.

He'd made the decision to reject any chance that the baby she carried might be his.

And not once in nine years had he ever doubted that conviction. He'd thought of Paige off and on through the years, but not once had he thought of the baby she'd carried. Of his son. Of Luke.

He'd been an idiot, not to mention the bastard that Paige had called him. The realization didn't fit and he was frowning by the time he and Luke finally found her, standing near the Ferris wheel, where they'd left her.

She looked so beautiful in her artfully faded jeans and expensive silk sweater, her hair blowing in the slight breeze working its way through the carnival. He had the urge to run his hands through it the way he used to, soaking up its softness as he leaned down to kiss her sweetly pink lips.

She was a far cry from the Paige Matthews who had left this town broke and alone, and for the first time he wondered how she'd made the transition. How she'd landed so firmly on her feet when most teenaged mothers without support systems usually sank deeper and deeper into hell.

He might have issues with the way things had gone down years ago, but he couldn't say that he had any complaints about how she had raised his very happy, very well-adjusted son to date. His concerns from a week ago—about her fitness as a mother—had all but disappeared.

As Luke ran ahead and gave her a hug, she laughed and squeezed him tightly against her. Logan felt himself grow hard at the sound of her laughter. At the incandescent joy on her face and the wide smile that stretched across her beautiful mouth. As he shifted, trying to adjust himself so his arousal wasn't so obvious, he was desperately afraid his animosity toward her was disappearing as well.

He knew better than to fall for her, knew better than to care about her in any context but as the mother of his child. They'd nearly destroyed each other once. He wasn't going to be party to that again.

And yet, as he moved closer to her, he found it nearly impossible to look away from her. There was something about her that touched him in a way he hadn't been touched in nine years, in a way his ex-wife had never managed to do.

She looked up as he approached and the smile on her face grew even wider. "So, you survived?"

Logan practically shook himself into coherence, forcing his thoughts from matters he shouldn't be contemplating and into the present. Everything would be so much easier if he maintained the status quo. "I did. It was touch and go for a few minutes, especially on the Witch's Wheel, but I muddled through."

"I'm so glad to hear that." She held out a drink container toward him. "I figured you'd be thirsty after all those rides, so I bought you a soda."

He felt his heart melt a little at the realization that she'd been thinking about him—even inadvertently—and his hand trembled as he reached to take the drink. His fingers brushed against hers and a jolt of electricity ripped through him. Suddenly, he was transported to when she used to wait for him after football practice, a huge, ice-cold water bottle in her hands. Back then, all he'd been able to think about was getting her alone. Today he was having the same problem.

"Thanks," he said. His voice came out huskier than usual, and from the darkening in her eyes, he knew Paige heard the difference. She didn't say anything though, just stepped away hastily.

"So," she said in a voice that was a shade too bright, "What should we do now?"

"I want to play some more games," Luke cried. "Dad promised to try to win me a fish again."

She glanced at him questioningly, and Logan tried to shake off his thoughts—and the arousal he was having more and more difficulty fighting. "I sure did. Point me in the right direction."

The rest of the carnival passed in a montage of

lights and dollar bills as Logan tried his best to win prizes for his son. He didn't win him a fish, despite spending enough money at the booth to buy ten fish from the local pet store, but he did win him a gigantic dog that the kid christened Roscoe almost as soon as his small, tan arms wrapped around its neck.

"He's a big *Dukes of Hazzard* fan," Paige said with a laugh. "During the school year, he DVRs the reruns and watches one every day when he's done with his homework."

"The kid's got good taste. That was one of my favorite shows when I was his age." He high-fived his son. "Luke and Bo Duke rock."

"I thought you'd be partial to Daisy."

"I always preferred blondes," he said jokingly, then stopped abruptly as the sensual tension between them ratcheted up another notch.

She didn't say anything for long moments, and it became obvious she was as lost in the past as he had been earlier. But she seemed to push it aside with an eye roll and a sassy little flip of her head. "What man doesn't?"

He might have left it at that, except as they worked their way toward the fairground exit, he saw the hurt she hadn't managed to hide lurking in the corners of her eyes.

He felt bad that a careless joke he hadn't even meant had hurt her and couldn't help wanting to make it right. But at the same time, he wasn't sure that was such a good idea. Things were shifting beneath his feet—beneath their feet—and he felt as though he balanced on the edge of a gigantic precipice. A wrong move would have him slipping and hurtling toward instant death.

And yet— "I didn't mean that the way it came out," he said as he pressed the button to unlock his truck's doors.

"Don't worry about it." Her voice was stilted, a surefire way to tell that he had, indeed, hurt her feelings. It was amazing how much he remembered from the old days, and how much came back to him the longer he was around her.

"Look, Paige, you weren't some faceless blonde to me. I…" He wasn't sure what he wanted to say to her. The kiss from the day before hung between them, along with all of the baggage from their past.

She waited for Luke to scramble into the backseat and put on his seat belt before she climbed in. "I mean it, Logan. It's no big deal. I guess I'm overly sensitive." She shook her head. "I had a great time tonight. Luke and I both did, so let's not let something stupid ruin our good moods."

He nodded slowly, not sure if she meant what she was saying but glad to be let off the hook so easily. "I had a really good time, too."

"I figured that out. Although how you could have

when you had to go on all those crazy rides, I'll never know."

"I considered it my initiation to fatherhood. I missed all the sleepless nights and dirty diapers, so this was the least I could do."

She didn't respond, and he didn't know what else to say, so he kept his mouth shut through the rest of the drive. They'd spent the first week sniping at each other, and now that that seemed to be gone, there was nothing to say. More accurately there was too much to say, but he didn't know where to begin.

When he pulled up in front of Penny's house, he half expected Paige to grab Luke and make a run for the door. Instead, she stuck around for a minute, even after a sleepy Luke headed inside.

"Would you like to come in for a little while?" she asked, almost shyly.

His arousal from the day before came back with a vengeance, making him so hard so fast that Logan wasn't sure he would be able to walk. But after more than a week of being relegated to the car or the front porch, he wasn't about to pass up a chance to see how Paige and Logan were living this summer.

As he climbed out of the truck, he told himself his curiosity stemmed from making sure his son had a healthy, happy home. But even he found that difficult to believe it, especially since his erection was pressed so hard against his fly that he feared he'd have permanent zipper tracks.

He wasn't going inside Penny's house because of his son. He was doing it because he wanted Paige Matthews more now than he ever had at eighteen.

## CHAPTER TWELVE

"CAN I GET YOU SOMETHING to drink?" Paige asked, as she let Logan in. "The place is a mess because of the construction, but we have lemonade, soda. I think Penny's also got some white wine in the fridge."

He glanced around. "Where *is* your sister?"

"She's spending a few days in Portland, hunting for some furniture to fill in the guest rooms we're almost finished with."

"You've already got some of the rooms finished?" he asked. "I'm impressed. You're a fast worker."

"I've been designing sets for years—changing them up with one or two days' notice if the director decides he needs to go another direction. Quick decorating is something of an art form for me."

"I guess so."

He didn't say anything else and she felt butterflies beating in her stomach as she struggled for something to say. Why had she asked him in? She didn't have the first idea of what to do with him now that he was standing in the foyer of her sister's house.

Thankfully, Luke chose that moment to make an

appearance at the top of the stairs. "Mom, my dog looks great sitting on my dresser. I'm going to leave him there all sum—" His voice cut off as he realized his father was standing next to her. "Dad! You came in."

"I did." Logan grinned at his son, an easy curving of his lips that somehow made her stomach even more nervous. What was happening to her? To them? She'd been content hating him.

He was looking at her differently, had been ever since he'd picked them up that afternoon. And now she was doing the same—thinking of how handsome he looked in his faded jeans and black T-shirt, instead of how much she resented the way he'd tossed her out of his life.

It needed to stop. She needed to stop it. Whatever she was thinking, whatever crazy emotions were zinging their way through her, had to stop. Logan was the father of her child, nothing more. She wouldn't let him be more, couldn't let him be more after everything that had happened between them.

Was he attractive? Absolutely—but he always had been. Attraction hadn't stopped him from tossing her out on her ear and it hadn't helped her in that first year away from Prospect when everything was so difficult, including finding a job that paid enough to put a leaky roof over her head and pay for prenatal doctor visits.

The thought of those long, lean months—years, really—had her moving toward the stairs at a near-run. She needed to put some distance between them, needed to get away from Logan for a few minutes, so that when she looked at him she didn't see the warmth in his eyes. She could only afford to see the ice-cold rage that had been directed at her all those years before. Anything else was emotional suicide. And she'd already been there, done that *and* had the T-shirt. It hadn't been a pretty ride.

"It's late, Luke. You need to take a quick shower and get all the dirt and sugar from the carnival off you and then go to bed."

"But, *Mooooooooom*—"

"No, *but, Mom* tonight," she answered firmly. "If you take a quick shower, we can read a chapter from your book before bed."

"A whole chapter?" he asked, delighted.

"A whole chapter," she agreed, heading up the stairs. Maybe Logan would get bored and take off before she was done.

"Can Dad read it to me?"

Paige paused on one of the steps, tried to cover the shocked hurt the request generated. But she must have done a lousy job of it because both guys started backpedaling.

"It's only because he's never seen my room, Mom.

And he's never read a book to me. I thought it would be fun, just this one time."

"That's okay," Logan said, holding up a hand. "I don't want to mess with anyone's routine. I'll head out now and see you the day after tomorrow for the baseball game, okay, Luke?"

He headed for the door and her son's face fell. His chest rose and fell rapidly and his expression told her Luke was trying hard not to cry. It made her feel petty. She'd come this far for her son—what was one more step toward the dark side if it made him happy?

"Don't be silly," she said, her voice sharp and stilted. She knew she sounded ridiculous, but there was nothing she could do about it. The fact that she was saying the words would have to be good enough for Logan.

"You can stay. I mean, if you want to. If you've got somewhere to go, I'm sure Luke and I would understand. But if you don't and you want to stay and read him a book, that would be fine with me. I mean—" She let out a huge sigh, forced herself to stop babbling. "Stay, Logan. It's fine."

He didn't answer for a few seconds, choosing instead to focus on her face. She tried to school her features into the appearance of neutrality, but must not have succeeded, because from the way he studied her, as though he found something interesting to stare at.

"All right," he finally agreed before heading up the stairs. "What book are we reading?" he asked, as Luke cheered.

"It's supercool. It's about this kid who went to basketball camp but everything goes wrong. His suitcase gets lost, and then he gets put on the worst team by mistake—or at least, he thinks it's a mistake. I'm not sure what else happens—we haven't gotten that far."

"We'll have to find out tonight. So, do you like basketball?"

"I love it. When I grow up, I want to be a basketball player." He paused, looked Logan over appraisingly. "I have to admit I was kind of hoping you'd be a little taller. Six-two is good, but not if you want to play pro ball."

Paige turned a laugh into a cough, but it was difficult—particularly considering the fact that Logan's eyes were brimming with amusement when he looked at her. Their child really was one of a kind.

"What position do you play?"

"I'm tall for my age, so I play center."

"Oh, yeah? Are you any good at it?"

"Yeah, I'm really good. Not, like, Shaq good or anything, but still I can hold my own."

This time Paige did laugh, and Logan joined in as

he ruffled Luke's curls. "You've got a great attitude, kid. That will take you far in life."

"That's what Mom says. In fact—"

Paige fired his pajamas at him, hit him square in the chest. "Mom says shower. Now. Or no book."

"Aw, Mom." He gave her his best puppy-dog eyes and for a second, she wanted to cave. Especially since as long as he was around, she had a buffer between her and Logan.

At the same time, she knew her son, could see the tiredness on his face. If she didn't get him showered and into bed in the next few minutes, he would turn into a total bear. And much as she would like to see how well Logan coped with him when he got like that, she didn't want to put Luke through the discomfort.

"I'll tell you what. I've already got the water running, so it should be nice and warm for you. You take the fastest shower on record—as long as everything that needs washing gets washed—and I won't hassle you about the not so vital stuff, like your hair. At least for tonight. Deal?"

"Deal!" Luke cried as he zipped into the bathroom, already pulling his shirt over his head.

Logan shook his head as he watched him go. "He's certainly a whirlwind, isn't he?" he asked when the bathroom door closed with a resounding thud.

"He keeps me on my toes."

"I have a feeling he'd keep my entire department on their toes."

"Well, he does have a lot of his mother in him."

As soon as the words slipped out, she wanted to call them back. She'd meant them as a joke, a way to diffuse some of the tension she was feeling, but Logan wasn't laughing. Instead, his eyes turned the deep silver of the moonlit waves she could hear crashing in the background, a surefire sign that he was taking her comment a lot more seriously than she had meant it.

Sure enough, he shoved a hand through his hair—a gesture she remembered from the bad old days as a sign of his agitation—and crossed the room until he was standing right next to her. "I wasn't saying that, Paige."

"I know you weren't," she answered with a smile. "I wasn't trying to snipe at you. I had a rough childhood. I got in trouble. I've never said otherwise."

"Yeah, but you weren't nearly as tough as most people thought you were, either."

"What about you?"

He raised an eyebrow? "What about me?"

"How tough did you think I was?"

The bathroom door flew open before he could answer, and Luke bounded out, dressed in his favorite superhero pajamas. "Book time! Book time!"

The look on Logan's face said he'd been saved by

the bell, but Paige couldn't help being a little disap-
pointed. Despite everything that had happened between them, despite all the ways he had hurt her in
the past, she had desperately wanted an answer to
that one question.

PAIGE'S QUESTION CIRCLED in his head, bouncing
around his brain long after she'd gone downstairs.
Even as he read chapter six of *The Adventures of
a Wanna-Be Basketball Player* to Luke, his mind
was filled with thoughts about that long-ago fight
between them.

He'd been an idiot to cut her out of his life so
harshly. A moron to hold on to his hurt so tightly that
it had blinded him to anything and everything else,
including the pain he was inflicting on Paige.

He'd cost Luke years when they could have been
together. But what if he'd cost himself more? What
if he'd cost himself a chance to be happy with Paige?
Who knows if they would have made it—seventeen
was way too young to be thinking about forever—but
he'd never even given them a shot. God, the hubris
of youth really was unbelievable.

Distracted, he didn't do a very good job of reading aloud, but Luke was too tired to complain. He
was asleep within four pages, his little face quiet and
serene for the first time since Logan had met him.

He knew he should leave, knew he should tuck his

son into bed then head downstairs, make some excuse to Paige. But he didn't do it. He couldn't. Tonight, there was nowhere else he would rather be than right here, with his son and with Paige. He wanted to hear her laugh again, to see her eyes sparkle with her special brand of infectious joy. It had been missing from his life for a long time, and it wasn't until recently that he'd even known that he'd missed it.

Which only made him a bigger idiot.

He wasn't sure how long he sat on the edge of the bed, watching Luke sleep. Counting the smattering of freckles across his nose. Cataloguing each small scar on his arms and hands, wondering what daredevil stunts his son had performed to get them.

He couldn't believe how beautiful Luke was—not only on the outside, but on the inside as well. The idea of letting him go at the end of the summer, of seeing him once a month or so after Luke and Paige returned to L.A., made him sick.

He wanted much more time than that. There were still so many things he wanted to show him. They hadn't been fishing yet or played baseball, hadn't hiked through the state parks in the area or built a model airplane. Two months wasn't enough time. But he doubted two years would be, either. Not after having missed so much.

His phone buzzed and he reluctantly pulled it out of his pocket, afraid that it would be work pulling him away from the best night he could remember having in a long time. But a quick glance at the screen showed him a text from his father.

Your mom wants you to have dinner with us tomorrow. I am not supposed to take no for an answer. Rudolfo's at 7 p.m.

Logan really had been banned from the house. He shook his head, wondering if he should be annoyed or amused. Rudolfo's was his mother's fallback meeting place and if he should screw up there, God only knew where he'd end up. Probably at the burger joint on the wrong side of town. Not that he was so sure that was a bad deal. He much preferred hamburgers to the food his mother prepared.

He wanted to say he couldn't believe the way she was behaving, but the fact of the matter was, he could. His mother was not known for her acceptance—at least not with anyone but his father. It was bad enough that he'd messed around with Paige when he was in high school. The fact that his illegitimate child had made a sudden appearance in town, thrusting his family into the limelight of unsavory gossip? That was not to be tolerated.

In this moment, sitting beside his sleeping son, coming off the high of his day, temporarily at peace with Paige, Logan wondered how much influence his mother had had on his intolerance nine years ago. An uncomfortable place to linger when he'd resented his mother's attitudes and considered himself a better person for being more accepting. Yet the evidence was overwhelming. There had been no acceptance or understanding or even listening as he'd belittled Paige that day.

And why not? It wasn't like the kid couldn't have been his—back then he had made love to Paige every chance he got. But by the time she told him about being pregnant, he'd been so opposed to believing she might be carrying his kid that he'd kicked her out of his life even though she swore that the baby was his.

Why had he done it? Because a friend of his had said that Paige had come on to him? Because a couple of football buddies had told him she'd slept with them as well? Even if she had, that hadn't negated his own culpability. Clearly.

Had he really believed his friends back then, or had he used their stories as an excuse to break up with a girl he cared about, a girl he loved, because his family and friends thought she was unsuitable for him. Oh, the guys she'd been with before him hadn't minded sleeping with Paige, but none of them had actually had a relationship with her—a fact that had been glaringly obvious once.

He'd told himself her past didn't matter, told her

that he understood—and he'd been sure that he had. But he'd been lying to himself. Maybe he had chosen to believe his friends because it was easier than dealing with the truth. That his football dreams, his career dreams, were over if he'd gotten a girl pregnant. He really hoped that hadn't been the case, because just the suggestion of it made him feel like the biggest asshole who had ever walked the earth. And more like his mother, who was selfish and all about appearances, than he'd thought possible.

It was a terrible feeling, especially as he thought of everything his kid had had to do without because his father had been too much of a jerk to even consider his mother's point of view.

There was a gentle knock on Luke's door, and he turned to see Paige, a questioning look on his face. "Is everything okay in here?"

"Yeah." He focused on the wall behind her head, embarrassed to face her after his realizations. "I was just looking at him."

She smiled. "I do that a lot. He's pretty amazing, huh?"

"He's incredible. I can't believe how much I already love him. I wish—" Paige wasn't the best one to voice his regrets to. She'd been the one who had been hurt most by the fallout between them, after all.

But she wasn't going to let it go. "What do you wish?"

"What was he like as a baby? As a toddler? Was he easy, or did he drive you nuts?"

Paige didn't answer right away, and at first he felt as though he'd overstepped his bounds. He'd tried to take things slow, to let things unfold naturally, but he was starved for information about his son. About Paige and their life in Los Angeles.

"Never mind. Look, I'll—"

"Do you want to see some of his baby pictures? I've got some saved on my laptop. Not many, but enough to give you an idea of what he was like."

"I—" It took a moment before he could force any words around the knot that seemed to have taken up residence in his throat. "I would really like that."

She nodded, then headed downstairs. After brushing a kiss on the top of Luke's head, Logan followed, feeling as though his entire world had narrowed to this house and the two people in it.

## CHAPTER THIRTEEN

WHAT THE HELL WAS SHE DOING? Paige wondered as she settled on the couch next to Logan and turned on her laptop. With the bottle of wine she'd gotten out earlier on the coffee table in front of them, and Luke's pictures a few keystrokes away, things suddenly seemed a lot more intimate than she'd wanted them to be.

She should have sent Logan home after he put Luke to bed. But he'd looked so lost sitting there next to their son, so desperate for information about him, that she hadn't been able to turn him away. Even her old standby argument—about how Logan deserved to miss out on Luke's life after what he'd done to her—seemed to fall flat in the face of his pain.

"I've taken a million pictures of him through the years, but most of them are in L.A. I can send them to you when I get home. But I always keep a file with my favorites on my computer—so I can look at them when I'm away from Luke."

"Do you have to be away from him a lot?"

She stiffened, sensing disapproval in the casual

question. "Not that much, actually. When he was younger he always traveled on location with me, but now that he's in school, he stays with a good friend of mine and her family. I'm usually gone only a couple of weeks—most of the actual set design can be done anywhere. I have to be around to supervise the construction on site before filming begins, but that's usually it. I've made a point of taking on jobs that are filming close to home or that don't require such extensive sets that I have to be away for months at a time."

"The set for *A Long Winter's Night* was incredible. I can't believe that didn't take months to build."

"It did. But Luke was younger then. He went with me to Australia. We had a great time."

"Do you have any of those pictures on here? I'd love to see them."

"I have a couple, actually." She clicked a few buttons and pulled up the file, then turned the laptop toward him. "Of us on the beach and near the Sydney Opera House—typical tourist stuff. But I also have some photos of us on location in the middle of the desert. He had a great time."

"I can imagine. Where else has he gone with you?"

"My first job actually building sets was in Vancouver. Lucas, the neighbor I told you about, got it for me. He was a huge set designer in his day—he won three Oscars for his work."

She waited for Logan to comment, but the slide show had started and he was engrossed in pictures of Luke as a baby. She hadn't had much money then—despite the fact that Lucas had let her live in the small guest house on his property for next to nothing—and all of Luke's clothes had come from a consignment shop down the street from where she waited tables.

Logan didn't say anything about the faded clothes though, and after a few minutes she figured out why. He didn't even see them—he didn't have eyes for anyone but Luke. It might have been sweet, if it didn't scare her so much. Made her worry about things like custody and mandatory visits—all the things she'd worked so hard to put out of her mind these past few days.

"How old was he here?" he asked, pointing to a picture of a chubby Luke on a blanket in the park.

"About four months, if I remember correctly. I'd had pneumonia, so we'd been cooped up in our little cottage for over a week and Luke was going stir-crazy. He was so happy to get out in the sunshine that day that he giggled for hours."

The look Logan gave her over the laptop was inscrutable. "You had pneumonia?"

"It was no big deal. Luke was young so I wasn't sleeping well and I got rundown." She shrugged it off, though those weeks when she'd been so sick had been some of the worst of her life. She'd barely been able to breathe, but had kept working, kept taking care of Luke, until she could hardly walk three steps without collapsing. Lucas had tried to help, but he was in his late seventies and there was only so much he could do with a baby before he got tired.

She'd made it through, had gotten her first set-designing job not long after that and everything had fallen into place in the next couple of years. She didn't need or want Logan to feel sorry for the girl she'd been, because she was quite proud of the woman that girl had become.

He must have registered her No Trespassing signs, because he didn't ask any more questions about that time, instead contented himself by clicking to the next picture. "Is this Disneyland?"

"Yeah. I saved up for months so that I could take Luke for his third birthday. He had so much fun—we both did."

"I can see that." He studied the photo of Luke in front of his favorite ride. "If his smile got any wider it wouldn't fit on his face."

"I know. That's why I love that picture."

He clicked to the next one.

"Oh, that's one from Australia. We spent a couple days at the beach after the set was finally done. We went snorkeling and I ended up getting stung by a jellyfish."

He looked up sharply. "You got stung?"

"Yeah, and it turns out I'm allergic to jellyfish. Who knew? It was awful—I swelled up like a balloon."

"That's terrible. Was someone around to help take care of Luke while you were recovering?"

His question, preceded by the others, got her back up. "I don't need anyone to take care of me, Logan. I've been doing it for as long as I can remember. And *I* took care of Luke." She flipped through the next half a dozen photos, all of which were taken after that day on the beach. "Does he look like he's suffering in those pictures?"

"That's not what I meant, Paige."

"Well, what did you mean?" She rose and started to pace. "You keep asking all these questions about who he stays with and who took care of him. I'm a good mom. I don't neglect my son."

"*Our* son. And of course you don't neglect him. If you thought that's why I was asking, then I'm sorry. I just want to know how you managed. Raising a kid with two parents is hard. I can't imagine what it would be like doing all this by yourself."

His simple apology deflated her anger, and she was left standing halfway across the room and feeling foolish. "No, I'm sorry for jumping down your throat. I'm a little touchy about Luke, as you can see."

"There's no reason for you to be. I have nothing but respect for what you've done. And I'm sorry—really sorry—that I left you alone to raise him by yourself."

Paige froze for a second, unsure if she'd heard Logan correctly. Her uncertainty must have shown on her face, because he grinned.

"You don't have to look so shocked, you know. I can apologize when I'm wrong. It doesn't make up for what you went through—what you both went through—but it's the best I can do at this point."

"It wasn't so bad," she answered, settling onto the couch next to him and continuing to flip through pictures until she got to the last one. For the first time since she'd come back to Prospect, she felt herself really relaxing—and wanting to confide in him about Luke.

"The first year was tough because I was young and broke and had no idea what I was doing. I remember trying so hard and failing miserably at almost everything I did. But once I got the hang of things, it got a lot easier. I got my GED and started taking a few classes toward my degree and Lucas got me into set designing. Luke got older and lately it's been pretty fabulous."

Logan didn't say anything, so she glanced up at

him, expecting to share a smile. Except he wasn't
smiling. His lips were pressed tightly together and
his eyes—usually so light—were nearly black and
filled with so much pain it took her breath away.

"Logan? What's wrong?"

He didn't answer, simply pulled her into his arms
and buried his face in her neck.

"Logan?" she asked again, her arms wrapping
around him instinctively.

"Thank you for having him. For taking such good
care of him when I was too big of a jerk to—"

"Hey." She pulled back enough to see his face. "I
think that's enough with the self-flagellation. While
I spent years dreaming of you saying all this to me,
the fact of the matter is, I could have called you and
I didn't. I could have given you a chance to be a part
of Luke's life before now, and I didn't. And that was
my mistake, so I'm sorry, too."

She waited for him to say something after her big
concession, but he didn't. Maybe because there was
nothing to say. Instead, he lowered his mouth to hers
in a kiss that was so sweet it took her, instantly, to
the very first time he'd kissed her.

They'd been at the beach right outside of town. It
had been winter, so it was cold and no one else was
around. She'd shivered and he'd pulled her against
him before lowering his lips to hers so softly that,

with her eyes closed, she couldn't be sure she wasn't imagining it.

That's how he kissed her now, with gentle touches of his lips to hers. Again and again, until her heart was pounding and her body aching for his. Knowing she couldn't take much more without screaming, she slid her hands up his back, tangled them in his hair, and brought Logan's mouth down on hers firmly enough to make them both cry out.

And then they were kissing, licking, biting, stroking, *devouring* each other with their mouths. He tasted so good—like spicy cinnamon and the strong, dark espresso she liked to drink by the gallon—that she wanted to go on kissing him forever, absorbing the flavors of him deep inside herself.

He must have agreed, because he didn't push for more, didn't try to take anything but her mouth. And when his tongue tangled with hers, she gasped. Opened herself fully to him. Gave herself to him the way she had so many times before.

Logan didn't wait for a second invitation. Levering himself over her, he trapped her against the sofa, caged her with one arm on either side of her as he pressed his upper body against her.

Paige moaned, arched her back, pressed herself more tightly to him in an effort to give her aching breasts some relief. It didn't work. The contact only made her hotter, made her want him more. Her nipples ached, and she wanted him to touch her there—needed him to touch her with a desperation that bordered on insanity.

But she was insane, crazy, absurd to contemplate doing this. She'd trusted Logan once, had given him everything, and had been left a broken, bloody shell of herself. It had taken her months to work her way from the precipice of depression he'd left her dangling over, years to get to where she was now—happy, confident, fulfilled.

If she followed through with this, if she let him make love to her as her body was screaming for her to do, where would that leave her in the morning? Once, Logan had been everything to her and he had nearly destroyed her. She didn't know if she could do that again, or if this time she would shatter into so many pieces she—like Humpty Dumpty in Luke's favorite nursery rhyme—would never be able to put all the pieces back together again.

Wresting her mouth away from Logan's, she pushed at his shoulders even as she longed to wrap her body around him and never let go. "No," she gasped. "I can't—"

The teenage Logan would have kept kissing her, would have tried to persuade her, but this Logan— the grown-up version—stopped instantly. He pulled back, slid off her until he was kneeling on the ground between her thighs, and simply looked at her.

His lips were swollen from her kisses and he was breathing even faster than she was. He was tense—like a jungle cat ready to pounce—his muscles hard as rock between her legs. And his eyes, his crazy, wonderful eyes were silver chaos as he stared at her, dark and swirling and heated and so tender, that she felt her breath catch in her throat.

And still he didn't push her, didn't pressure her. Stayed where he was and watched her, cataloguing every shaky breath she took. She should apologize, tell him to go, tell him she wasn't ready for this. For him.

But she couldn't, not while desire was a throbbing wound between them. Not while the past was a shuddering presence all around them and tomorrow was a future too distant to think about.

It had been nine years since she'd trusted a man to touch her intimately, nine years since she'd trusted *this* man not to hurt her. Could she do it again?

Reaching out she stroked her fingers over his forehead, down his cheek, across his eyes. His lashes fluttered, his eyelids drifting shut and she marveled at the trust it took for him to be so vulnerable. She had yet to close her eyes with him, wasn't sure if she'd ever be able to again.

But as her trembling fingers drifted across his mouth, he kissed them—one after the other—and she knew she had to try. It might be the stupidest thing she'd ever done, certainly the dumbest thing she'd done in the past nine years, but she couldn't help it. She wanted him, needed him, and tonight she would take him. If, in the morning, it proved to be a mistake, then she would deal with those consequences, too. But she would take this moment with Logan, with the only man she had ever loved, and say to hell with the future.

HE FELT THE MOMENT PAIGE gave in, the moment she stopped fighting the emotions that were swelling between them like a tsunami. Part of him wanted to take her right then, when her defenses were down. To thrust himself into her graceful, giving body and lose himself the way he had so many, many times before.

But he needed to be sure—needed her to be sure—even more than he needed to be inside her. She mattered to him. Even after all this time and all the anger and pain that had gone before, she mattered and he needed her to know that.

"Are you sure?" he whispered against her fingers, resisting the urge to suck them—one at a time—into his mouth.

She shook her head no, but whispered, "I want to be with you, Logan. I want to feel you inside me. I want to know that it's you holding me, you taking me."

Her words shot straight through him, making him

even harder though he hadn't thought it was possible. Pure, unadulterated lust grabbed him in a stranglehold, made every breath he took an agony.

"Oh, darlin'," he said as he lowered his mouth to hers, "So do I. So. Do. I."

He pulled her closer, forced her legs wider, until he was nestled right against her sex. He could feel the heat of her even through the denim of their jeans, and it took every ounce of willpower he had not to strip her and take her right there on the family room couch.

But there was Luke to think of, Luke who might come out of his bedroom looking for his mom or a glass of water or a midnight snack.

Leaning forward, he brushed his lips over the corner of her mouth, swept his tongue over her dimple again and again. She tasted so good. "Where's your bedroom?" he asked intently, determined to get her off the couch before he was so far gone he no longer cared.

"I'm sharing with Luke right now."

He cursed under his breath, long and low and mean. She laughed, a breathy sound that shot straight to his sex. "There's a guest room that's almost finished. It doesn't have any furniture yet, but there's a mattress in there. Is that okay?"

He half-snorted, half-laughed. A mattress on the floor sounded like heaven to him right now. Of course, in this state he'd be more than willing to make do with the floor, a wall, the bathroom counter. Anywhere he could get inside her, quickly, was more than all right with him.

He didn't say that, though—she was already nervous and he didn't want to make it worse by coming on like a starving man. But he was starving, desperate for the sight and sound and taste and smell of her. Delirious with the need to touch every inch of her.

"It's perfect," he said, forcing himself to stop running his lips over her satiny skin. "Which way?"

She led him up the stairs, her curvy ass swinging a little with each step she took. Torture. Pure, unadulterated torture.

His lips found hers and delivered hot, drugging kisses that made her quiver and made him need. The second they reached the bedroom, he shoved open the door, propelled her inside. He followed right behind her, crowding her, pushing her gently but inexorably toward the wall. Bracketing her with his arms as he leaned forward and took her mouth, one more time, with his own.

The kiss took him right over the edge and then he was devouring her, his mouth and teeth and tongue all working together to absorb her into him. Her mouth was dark and wild and sweet and so addicting that he wasn't sure he would ever be able to let her go.

Didn't know how he had ever been stupid enough to let her go the first time he'd had her.

Desperate to feel her, he ripped her sweater over her head. She gasped and her head fell back on her shoulders. She was peaches and cream, light and shadow, salvation and debauchery all rolled into one. He'd never seen anything more beautiful than her in the moonlight streaming through the window.

Tracing his thumb over her lavender lace bra, he moved his fingers over the inviting swell of her breast. He lingered there, savored the incredible softness of her skin beneath his calloused fingers then moved farther, until his whole palm rested flat against her breastbone. Collaring her, possessing her.

"Say you want this." He ground the words out as his fingers stroked the pulse beating wildly in her throat. "Say you want me."

"I want this," she whispered, her eyes cloudy with desire. "I want you."

She brought her hand up, wrapped it around his. Lifted his fingers to her parted lips and kissed each one of them before slipping his index finger deep into her mouth and laving it with her tongue.

He nearly lost it right there, nearly ripped her jeans down her legs and took her against the wall. Only the fact that this was their first time together in so very long kept him sane. Only the fact that he wanted to, needed to, make this special for her kept him from taking her like a wild man.

She relinquished his finger slowly and he groaned, desperate to be back inside the moist heat of her mouth. Desperate to feel that warmth licking down his body to his sex.

But that could come later—much later. Right now he needed to feel her skin against his.

Keeping her pinned with his body, he yanked off his shirt, then slid his hand up her back to unfasten her bra. She gasped as he slid it off her, nearly sobbed when his hands moved over her sides to cup the lush ripeness of her breasts.

The feel of her in his palms was so delicious, so right, that for a second he couldn't function. Leaning forward, he closed his eyes and rested his forehead against hers. Tried to calm down a little so that their lovemaking wasn't over before it began.

It almost worked, until he realized that he was breathing her exhalations, that with each breath he took he was drawing her deeper and deeper into his body. The thought sent another wave of heat crashing through him and he brought his lips to her ear, nipped at her lobe—not hard enough to hurt, but firmly enough to have her back arching and her delicious breasts pressing more firmly into his hands.

Nothing he'd ever done—no adrenaline rush from chasing a bad guy, no endorphin rush from sex—had prepared him for his reaction to her. Not only the way his body caught fire when she was near him, but the way his heart trembled in his chest. The way he wanted to take care of her, apart from Luke. The way he wanted to bury the past, forget old hurts and move forward with her at his side. To hell with what everyone thought.

Control, he told himself, as he licked his way down her neck to the hollow of her throat and took the scent of lilacs deep inside.

Control, he reminded himself as he skimmed his lips over the pale undersides of her breasts and nipped gently at her.

Control, he promised himself as he pulled one hard, sweet nipple into his mouth and began to suck.

She screamed, a hot, strangled little sound. He decided control was highly overrated.

And then her hands were in his hair, tugging him to her hungry mouth. It was her turn to explore him, to run her tongue over his lips as she squeezed his shoulders. Smoothed her hands over the sensitive skin of his lower back. Cupped his ass and ground against him.

That's when he knew that no matter how much he wanted this to last, no matter how hard he tried to take things slowly, it wasn't going to happen. Not

DESERVING OF LUKE

now. Not when his body was literally starved for the feel of hers.

Pulling away from her, he started on her jeans, his fingers clumsy with desire as he tried to yank the zipper down. He fumbled once, twice, like the high school kid he'd been the last time he'd made love to her and she laughed.

"I'll do it." She was breathless, the words barely audible as she ripped off her jeans and shimmied them over her hips and down her thighs before letting them fall to the ground beside her.

Overwhelmed by a sudden need to see her—really see her—he moved his hand along the wall until he bumped into a light switch. Muttering a prayer that they'd gotten around to putting light bulbs in, he flipped it on and nearly trembled in delight when a soft glow flooded the room.

"You're so beautiful, Paige. So damned beautiful it takes my breath away." And she was, standing there wearing nothing but a pair of lavender panties. Her breasts were full and round, her hips lush, her legs long and toned. She was every late-night fantasy he'd had in the past nine years, every unfulfilled dream he'd woken from, hard and sweaty and desperate.

And she was here, in front of him. His for the taking.

"Not so beautiful," she answered. "I have…" Her

hand went to her flat stomach, to the light stretch marks that stretched across the skin. "From Luke."

He dropped to his knees, nuzzled his way across her belly as he imagined what it would have been like to touch her while his child nestled there.

Running his tongue along the edge of her bikini panties, he delved down below the elastic band and stroked his tongue over her mons.

She moaned, her eyes going wide as her fingers clutched at his hair. He repeated the action, looking up from beneath his lashes at her as he did. Her head was back, her lips parted, her eyes half closed and glowing. Her skin was flushed a dusky apricot and her body was trembling with each breath she took.

"Yes, beautiful," he said firmly. "The most beautiful thing I've ever seen."

Then he ripped off her panties.

# CHAPTER FOURTEEN

PAIGE SHUDDERED AS HER PANTIES ripped, bit her
tongue to keep from crying out when Logan thrust
his hand between her legs and cupped her. It had
been so long since she'd been touched by him and it
felt so good that, for a second, she wasn't certain her
legs would hold her.

Reaching out, she grabbed his shoulders. "Logan,
please."

"Please what, darlin'? Please stop or please keep
going?"

"I don't know. I need…"

"What? What do you need?"

"You." She moved a hand to his chin, tilted his
face until he was looking straight into her eyes. "I
need you."

"I was hoping you'd say that."

"Were you?"

"I was. Because I need you."

His words shot a thrill straight through her, had
her hands clutching at him as her knees did, indeed,
buckle, and she ended up on the floor beside him.

His laugh was wicked. "Am I going too fast for you?"

"You're going too slow."

She reached for him, started to unbutton his jeans but couldn't resist rubbing her palm against him. He jerked, cursed a little, but didn't move her hand. She grew bolder, cupping him through the thick fabric and stroking him with her thumb.

"Take my jeans off," he growled, thrusting against her hand.

She didn't have to be asked twice. After working his button through the hole, she unzipped his jeans slowly, enjoying every second of the job. Loving the vibrant heat of him beneath her palms and the dark sensuality of the look he was giving her.

When the zipper was finally down and she could no longer torture him with "accidental" brushes of her knuckles against him, she wiggled her hands inside his waistband and began pulling the denim down.

The jeans were baggy, so she shouldn't have had any trouble getting them off, but it took forever as she kept getting distracted by his heavy erection, so close to her cheek and mouth. Finally, unable to resist, she leaned forward and brushed her cheek against the burning, velvet length of him.

His shaft jerked in response, his hands tightening in her hair, so she did it again, this time blowing a little to torture him. Nine years was a long time, but not so long that she'd forgotten what he liked.

"I want to feel your hands on me." He ground the words out. "Now, Paige. Touch me. Please."

His voice was hoarse, rough, dark and dangerous. She was getting wetter, hotter, her body on the brink of an orgasm though he had barely touched her. But this was Logan. *Logan.* And she couldn't pretend to hate him any longer.

For months after she'd left Prospect, she'd dreamed of him touching her, holding her, loving her. She would wake up clutching her pillow and crying for him, her body on the brink of coming from dreams and memories alone. It was almost shocking to realize that this wasn't a dream, and Logan was here and she was touching him as she'd wanted to for far too long.

Unable to resist, she reached for him. Stroked him. Slid her hands over and around him, reveling in the feel of him and the desperate, hungry sounds coming from his throat. He was hotter than she remembered, thicker and her body ached with the need to feel him inside her.

LOGAN LET PAIGE stroke him as long as he dared, but when he felt himself getting too close to losing control, he tugged her hand away from him. She started to protest and he silenced her by lowering his mouth to her nipple, loving the way she tasted and the way her back arched at the first touch of his mouth.

A moan escaped her and she clutched at him, stroking him in one last, lingering caress that set every nerve ending in his body to jangling. In response, he used his tongue and his teeth to stroke and nibble as he sucked.

She gasped, trembled, her legs falling open. He took advantage of the situation, slid his hand up the inside of her thigh and brushed his knuckles against her. She was soft and wet, and so hot. He wanted to touch her, to taste her, to sink his body into hers and never leave. He wanted to make her come, wanted to feel her climax against his hand, his mouth.

Unable to resist the temptation any longer, he slid one long finger inside her and began to stroke. She moaned again, louder this time, and he leaned over her to capture the sound with his mouth.

He loved kissing her, always had. When they were kids he had kissed her for hours, reveling in the feel of her lips beneath his and the soft sounds of desire she always made. He stroked his tongue across the seam of her lips before drawing her lower lip between his teeth and sucking firmly.

Her eyes flew open, but they were a hazy, opaque green that told him she was as close to losing control as he was. He didn't let go, didn't stop kissing her, didn't rush for the prize as he would have at eighteen.

Instead, he took his time, savoring her mouth and the expressions—stark and real—flitting across her face.

He couldn't look away from the emotion there, couldn't get over the trust she was giving him after everything that had come before. Determined to make this good for her—to satisfy her—he set about making her as insane as she had already made him.

Curling his tongue around her nipple, he sucked at her until she was sobbing, trembling, crying out for him as her hips pistoned against his hand. He slid a second finger inside her, stroking the soft, hard bud at the apex of her thighs as he did, and she screamed.

Her inner muscles clamped around him and her head thrashed. Her hips came off the floor, and he took the opportunity to press kisses down her belly to her sex, alternating between long, lingering licks and quick, teasing little bites that had her clutching at his hair and chanting his name.

"Logan, please," she cried. "I can't take it, I can't take it. Logan, please!"

He slid down her body, pressed his face against her and inhaled the sweet, musky scent of her. And then set about driving Paige Matthews out of her mind.

SHE WAS OUT OF CONTROL, her body so desperate for completion that Logan could do anything to her—anything—and she would probably allow it. Need was a fiery maelstrom inside her, raking through her with each rapid beat of her heart. And when he lowered his mouth to her, began to lick, she knew that he was going to burn her alive.

She'd never felt this way before, had never felt this alive, this beautiful, this wanted. When they were young, Logan had taken his time with her, had made sure she was satisfied, but nothing of those long ago sessions could compare to this heat, this passion. This power that he seemed to have over her.

She arched toward him and he blew against her, the hot air sending tremors of pleasure soaring through her. She was close, so close, to something truly incredible and she wanted to go there, but she didn't want to go alone. She wanted Logan with her every step of the way.

"Please," she begged again. "I need you inside me. I need you with me—"

"I will be. I promise. Just relax and let me take care of you for a little while."

His tongue stroked over her again and again, light and hard, teasing and so wild that she couldn't stay still. She thrashed beneath him, her body under his thrall. Her lungs were burning, her body screaming, her heart beating so fast. It scared her a bit—she'd spent so much of the past nine years making sure she was the one in control. But the fear wasn't enough to make her stop him, wasn't enough to combat the insidious pleasure that had taken over every part of her.

The tension built and built inside her, a powerful wave taking her higher and higher. It was frightening and exhilarating and she clutched at Logan, needing something to hold on to. Needing him to keep her safe.

He chose that moment to reach up and stroke his thumb across her nipple, once, twice, and that added sensation, that added heat, was all it took. She shattered, her body bowing as wave after wave of her climax ripped through her from head to toe.

Suddenly, Logan reared back and fumbled a condom out of his wallet. Then he was thrusting inside her, and she reveled in the feel of him. But it took a few seconds for him to push himself all the way in. Once he was there, so deep she swore she could feel him in every part of her, Paige wrapped her arms and legs tightly around him and rode out another climax.

Logan gasped as Paige lifted herself against him and he wanted nothing more than to pound into her with every ounce of strength he had. But she was so tight, so incredibly tight, that he worried about hurting her.

Pulling back slowly, he thrust forward again, trying to be as gentle as his raging blood would let him. But Paige would have none of it. She dug her nails into his back, sank her teeth into his shoulder, tightened her legs around his waist so that he moved deeper.

She lifted her head, licked him from the center of his chest to the hollow of his neck and he knew he was lost. His hips pistoned forward, picking up a hard, quick rhythm that made his head swim and his body scream for completion. Flames licked over his skin, sizzled through his body, burned him alive as he thrust into her. Through it all, he focused on her, watched her face, lost himself in the pleasure washing over her.

Nothing had ever been as good as this.

Paige called out his name, grabbed on to him, and that was all it took to send him over the edge. Release tore through him, spreading through his whole body, sizzling and scorching along his nerve endings, roaring in his ears and his mind until all he could feel was Paige. Until all he knew was Paige.

He pumped faster, and felt her climax hit her as her body spasmed around his own. Then he was falling, spinning, shattering and for one blinding moment he was afraid that he wouldn't survive the pleasure. It was too intense, too all-consuming, too overwhelming.

He fastened his mouth onto Paige's, lost himself in the taste and feel of her and let himself go.

HE DIDN'T KNOW HOW LONG IT was before he came back to himself, before he could force his burned-out brain to form a coherent thought. "We didn't actually make it to the mattress," he said, idly playing with a few strands of Paige's hair.

She laughed, and since he was still inside her, the sound rolled through him and set off sparks all over again. He knew he should get off her, knew he was too heavy for her, but he couldn't force himself to move. Not yet. Not when he was still reveling in how good it felt to be inside Paige again.

"I can't say that I noticed."

"Neither did I. But then I wasn't on the bottom."

"Speaking of which…" She shoved at his shoulders until he rolled off her. As he pulled out, he was shocked at the immediate feeling of loss he felt, almost as if he wanted to spend his whole life curled up against Paige, loving her.

The thought sent him bounding to his feet. Not a place he wanted to explore. "Does that bathroom work?" he asked.

"Yeah."

"Then I'll be right back."

"And I'll be right here."

Paige watched Logan go, shocked at how awkward he had suddenly seemed. It didn't make sense to her, as she felt wonderful. Amazing. As if she could take on the world and win.

Scooting over to the mattress, she pulled the sheet off and wrapped it around herself as she waited for him to come back. She knew she should clean herself up as well, but she didn't want to. She wanted to stay here for a few minutes and bask in the incredible looseness of her body.

The second the bathroom door opened, however, she knew there would be no basking. Logan looked a little out of place and a lot confused. It gave her a pang, made her realize that he might not have felt the same way about their lovemaking as she had. Not that that was necessarily a surprise—she'd learned that lesson nine years ago, just a bit too late. But learn it she had, and she wouldn't be making the same mistakes tonight. The trick was not to look him in the eye.

Climbing to her feet, the sheet still clutched around herself, she handed him his pants. "If you need to be somewhere, I understand. Don't feel like you need to stick around—"

"Are you kicking me out?" He sounded incredulous.

"No. I figured you might need to go. You are the sheriff, after all, and you might be on call or something—"

"I'm not."

"Oh. Okay." She reached for her shirt, started to

shrug into it, but Logan stopped her with a hand on her arm.

"What's going on here, Paige?" He sounded confused and slightly angry and that set her own anger soaring. What did he have to be upset about? He was the one who had started acting like he couldn't get away from her fast enough.

"Nothing. You seemed…anxious to leave. I didn't want you to feel like you had to stick around."

He yanked on the sheet until she lost her grip. "And what if I want to stick around?" he asked. "Is that okay with you?"

Her heart trembled in her chest, more vulnerable than she liked to admit. What was it about this man that made her behave so foolishly? That made her want to give him everything even when she knew it wouldn't turn out well?

"That's fine with me."

"Good." He grabbed her around the waist and tumbled her to the mattress. "Because I'm not quite done with you yet."

"Oh, really?" She forced herself to raise an eyebrow instead of jumping for joy. "What else is there for you to do to me?"

"Oh, Paige. I've barely gotten started."

He lowered his mouth to hers, started to kiss her, but then pulled back at the last second. "I'm sorry. I don't know how you normally handle this. Do you want me to leave in a few hours, before Luke wakes up? Or should I stay? What do you usually do?"

For one long second, she didn't know how to answer him. She certainly couldn't tell him that the situation had never come up before, that he was the only man she'd slept with in almost a decade. He wouldn't believe her and telling him would serve no purpose except to make them both feel awkward.

She should probably tell him to leave before Luke woke up, but she didn't really want to do that. She wanted to sleep in his arms, wanted to wake up next to him—even if it was only for this one night. Luke was a late sleeper. Logan would probably be at work before her son even opened his eyes for the day.

Wrapping her arms around his neck, she whispered, "Stay," before taking his lips with her own. Tomorrow would come soon enough, and with it the consequences of this impetuous, impractical and absolutely amazing night. For now, she would concentrate on making this night last a long, long time.

## CHAPTER FIFTEEN

"You DIDN'T ANSWER YOUR father's text last night."
Logan's mother's voice, frostier than usual, came out
of his cell phone as Logan was pulling away from
the drive-through at the local bakery. He'd woken up
starving, and after deciding he wasn't about to rum-
mage around in Paige's kitchen—at least not until she
invited him—he'd hit on Delilah's as a great place to
pick up a casual, morning-after breakfast.

He'd had a few moments of concern when faced
with what kind of pastry to buy—it had been nine
years, after all, and he didn't have a clue if Paige's
tastes were the same. In the end, he'd ordered a whole
bakery box worth of stuff, figuring Luke could start
in on anything his mother didn't like.

"I was going to stop by later today and talk to
you," he answered. Which was true, though he *had*
been putting it off. He knew his mother was going to
have a million questions about Luke—and twice that
many opinions—and he hadn't been ready to deal
with it. Not yet, when he didn't have the answers to
many of those questions himself.

"Were you?" He winced at the fury in her tone. "What about?"

"Come on, Mom. Let's not play this game. You know you want to have your say about Luke."

"Is that my grandson's name? Luke?"

"It's short for Lucas, but yes. That's his name."

"I see. And how long have you known about Luke?"

"Not very long. I—"

"He's eight years old, from what I understand. How long is *not very long?*"

"Come on, Mom. I know you're upset, but I'm not really up for the inquisition this morning."

"Well, then, I suppose you should have thought of that and stopped by before the entire town has phoned me about a grandchild I didn't even know existed before last week."

Luke sighed in frustration. "It's not like I knew he existed either, Mom. I haven't been keeping him a secret for eight years, you know."

She sniffed. "How long have you been keeping him a secret?"

"I'm not. I haven't been."

"Then why haven't you been by to see me? Why have I had to be the one to call you—twice—about him?"

"Because my whole life doesn't revolve around you! I just found out about him a little over a week ago and I've been trying to wrap my head around the fact that I'm a father ever since. Should I have stopped by to talk to you and Dad earlier? Maybe. But we spoke last week, right after Paige got to town, and I wanted to have some answers before I talked to you again. It's taken me a little while to figure some stuff out. I mean, I just found out I have a son, Mom."

She was silent and for a second he thought he'd reached her. His mom could be tough, cold and un-emotional, but surely even she could understand how shocked he had been to find out about Luke. How his entire life had been thrown into a tailspin.

But then she spoke again, and he realized that no matter how many impassioned pleas he delivered, she wasn't going to see past the shock and embarrassment she had felt when the first phone call came in and she'd had no idea what her friend was talking about.

"And have you figured things out?" she demanded. "You and that…girl you used to date."

"Her name is Paige, Mother."

"I am aware of what her name is, Logan. I don't happen to care. Now answer the question."

His patience slipped another notch. He couldn't stand when his mother got like this—all high and mighty, where her emotions were the only ones that mattered. "What question is that?" he demanded, though he remembered very well what she'd asked.

"Have you figured out what you're going to do about this…situation?"

"He's not a situation. He's my son!" he told her as he pulled onto the highway that would take him to Paige's. "And what I'm doing is taking it slow. Getting to know him."

"Getting to know him. Really? After eight years?" Her voice dripped disgust.

"It's better than if it was after twenty years."

"I'm not so sure about that. And this woman, this Paige Matthews, asked anything from you yet?"

"I assume you mean money?"

"Well, I wasn't referring to Tiddly Winks."

"She hasn't asked for anything, Mom. And she won't. That's not what this is about."

"That's what you think. It's always about money in situations like this, Logan. Always. That girl left here with nothing and now that she's back, she'll be determined to get what she feels she deserves."

"That isn't true. But even if it was, so what?" He pushed harder on the accelerator, wanting to get to Paige's quickly so he had an excuse to end this ridiculous farce of a conversation with his mother. And she wanted to know why he hadn't called her right away? Because all she did was accuse and insinuate until he wanted to bang his head against the wall.

"He's my son and I am responsible for him. I

want to contribute to raising him—monetarily and otherwise. There's nothing wrong with that."

"Oh, Lord, she's got her hooks into you already."

That was it. He couldn't take any more. "Look, Mom, I need to go now. I'm due into work in a little while and I have to shower and change—"

"You're not running away that easily. At least tell me you haven't slept with her again."

He smiled as he flashed to what he and Paige had spent most of the past night doing. He wouldn't exactly call it *sleeping,* but he doubted his mother would be amused if he pointed that out to her. Besides, he didn't want to talk about that aspect of his relationship with Paige—not to anyone and certainly not to his mother.

But she must have read something into his prolonged silence, because he could all but hear her eye roll. "Oh, Logan, you know better than that. I told you nine years ago that girl was no good for you and here you are again, falling right into her trap."

"I don't know what you're talking about."

"Of course you don't. You're a man. You don't understand how women like that think."

"And you do?"

"Of course, sweetheart. How do you think I've dealt with your father's affairs through the years? His women practically came out of the woodwork for a while there, all of them after the same thing. I took care of them discreetly and I can take care of Paige as well, if you'll let me."

Shock ricocheted through him—not at the knowledge that his father had had a series of affairs, because as he'd gotten older he'd figured that out on his own. It was one of the reasons he'd been so insane when he found out Paige had been cheating on him. He'd loved her but not enough to be with her when he obviously wasn't enough for her. He'd spent his life watching his father chase after other women, seen how his lack of interest had hurt his mother, and had been determined—even at eighteen—not to let that happen to him.

But he hadn't known his mother *took care* of the women. What kind of ice circulated in her veins that she not only remained married to her hound dog of a husband, but also dealt with the woman he'd preferred over her?

"Why did you put up with it?" he asked because he couldn't stop himself. "Why did you stay with him if you knew he could never be faithful?"

"My dear boy, there is a lot more to a marriage than sexual fidelity. Your father might have tomcatted around with all those women, but who has he always come home to? Who has he been married to for thirty-five years?"

"And is that enough?" he asked. He knew he was

overstepping his bounds, but he couldn't help it. After everything that had happened between him and Paige he wanted another person's opinion. Someone who had experienced the same kind of betrayal he had at the hands of someone she loved. "Is it enough that he comes home after he's been with another woman? Doesn't it hurt, Mom, knowing where he's been and what he's been doing?"

There was a long silence on the other end of the phone, so long that he pulled the phone away from his ear to make sure she hadn't hung up on him. But she hadn't, so he waited her out. He knew he was pushing her, hurting her, but he needed to hear her answer.

"Of course it hurts," she whispered. "At first, you're in shock because you can't believe he would do something like that to you. You weep and you rage and he promises that it won't happen again. But it does, again and again, and every time he comes home and you know—you know—it's a new knife in your stomach. You make excuses for them and blame yourself—if I'd been a better wife, if he wasn't so stressed at work, if he felt like he could talk to me, then he wouldn't do this anymore. And you stick around through all of it because you have kids with him, because you love him, because you think you can change him.

"But here's a word of advice for you, Logan." Her

voice grew harsh, ugly. "You can never change the people you love. You can never make them into who you want them to be versus who they really are. And if there's one thing I've learned from my marriage and from the marriages of my friends, it is that once a cheater, always a cheater. And so you end up living with it, throwing your life away on someone who doesn't deserve you and who can never love you the way that you want to be loved."

His hands grew sweaty at her words, his stomach plummeting to his toes. Because he knew what she was talking about, knew what she was feeling. Hadn't he spent the past few days making excuses to himself for Paige's previous infidelities? Hadn't he told himself that she'd been young, confused, looking for attention from parents who didn't give a damn?

His stomach rolled and for one alarming second he thought that he was going to be sick right there in the middle of the highway. But he battled the nausea as he turned onto the driveway that would lead him to Paige. To Luke.

"I'm sorry, Mom. I didn't know." It was a lame thing to say, but he couldn't think of anything else. And he was sorry, sorrier than he could ever tell her for the pain she'd endured for thirty-five years.

"I don't want my life for you, Logan. I don't want you to spend years waiting by a window, wondering where your wife is and who she's with. You're better than that."

"I—" He wasn't sure what he wanted to say to her, wasn't sure what there was too say.

"It's all right. I understand." She cleared her throat and suddenly her voice, and their conversation, returned to normal. "Think about what I said, Logan. She won't change and you don't want to throw your life away on a woman who makes you feel like second best."

She clicked off, leaving him sitting in his truck outside his lover's house and wondering which end was up. Was his mother right? he wondered as he got out of the truck. Was Paige always going to be that girl who had cheated on him? When they'd been together, he'd been willing to give up his friends for her. To defy his parents for her. To do anything to make her understand that, despite her family, she belonged somewhere. That she belonged with him.

He'd thought he'd convinced her, but then she'd cheated on him anyway. Not because she'd fallen in love with someone else, but because she could. Because there were guys available who found her attractive and were more than willing to take her up on what she was offering.

There would always be men who found her attractive—Paige was a beautiful, vibrant woman. There would always be men who would sleep with her, married or not. Mother or not. Could he live with that? With the uncertainty of not knowing where she was or what she was doing? Or could he, God forbid, live with knowing exactly what she was doing and who she was doing it with?

He got out of the truck slowly, picking up the coffees and bakery box as he went. It was strange to think of how amazing he'd felt when he'd been with Paige last night, how right it had felt to be inside her again. That mood seemed a million miles away now. As he let himself into the silent house he wondered what he was doing here.

Was he stupid to open himself up to Paige again? He'd loved her years ago and she had shattered his entire world. Now she was back, with his son in tow, and he had let her in. Had given her the means to destroy him all over again.

Maybe it would be different if he really thought she'd changed. But last night, when he'd asked her if he should leave, she'd been fine with him staying. Fine with him spending the night. Fine with Luke finding him in her bed in the morning. It had shaken him then, the realization that she might have done this many times before. That she had let men spend the night and have breakfast with his son in the morning.

He'd told himself it didn't matter—it wasn't as though he'd been celibate since she'd left. He'd had numerous girlfriends, had even married someone else, for God's sake. But he wasn't holding the number of lovers she had against her—he really wasn't. Only the ease with which she brought them into his son's life.

He took a sip of his much-anticipated coffee, but it tasted too bitter and he spat it into the sink. Bitter like he felt. Bitter like he was very afraid he would become if he stayed with Paige.

Maybe he was moving too quickly, assuming too much. He should talk to her—he was smart enough to know that he needed to explain his concerns, find out if he was off base with his assumptions. Yet, even as he knew that, he'd learned at an early age not to ask a question if he didn't want to hear the answer. Right now, with Paige, he was very afraid.

Everything he'd done with Paige last night, all the ways he'd tried to satisfy her in the past, which hadn't been enough…and his mother's words came back to him.

*She won't change and you can't change her.*

*Left alone, sitting by the window.*

*Wondering why you weren't enough.*

The walls started to close in on him and Logan knew he had to get out. He couldn't stay here any longer, not with the past a living, breathing animal clawing away at his insides. Not with all of his hopes and dreams—hopes and dreams he'd barely been aware of having—lying shattered at his feet.

If he stayed here, he'd just end up back upstairs, in bed with Paige as he desperately tried to convince himself that she was his. Desperately tried to convince himself that the past wouldn't repeat itself.

No, he needed to be alone for a while. Grabbing his keys, he bounded out the door. He needed to get away for a while. Needed to be by himself. Needed to think. He had to decide, once and for all, if he could trust Paige not to hurt him again.

## CHAPTER SIXTEEN

PAIGE WOKE UP ALONE.

Sleepy, satisfied, more than half in love with Logan again and thinking about a morning quickie before he had to go to work, Paige reached across the mattress to where she expected him to be, only to find the space empty.

Logan was probably in the bathroom or had run downstairs to make coffee before work. She rolled over, luxuriating in the stretch to well-used, slightly sore muscles. She buried her face in his pillow, absorbing the sexy ocean and pine tree scent of him.

She could wake up this way every day for the rest of her life.

The thought had her eyes flying open, had her sitting up in bed and clutching the sheet to her chest as an unfamiliar feeling of vulnerability worked its way through her. She hadn't really been thinking that, had she? Hadn't really been imagining waking up next to Logan every day for the rest of her life.

She couldn't have been. Even the thought was absurd, the idea that they could somehow make things work, after everything that had happened between them.

Except that she was. She really was.

She was being ridiculous, she told herself. One night did not a lifetime make. But nothing with her and Logan had ever been just one night. And the way he'd held her, the way he'd made love to her over and over again, the way he'd wrapped himself around her and slept with her head pressed into his heart—it had to mean something to him. It certainly meant a lot to her. Maybe too much.

Shoving her wayward bangs from her face, Paige crawled out of bed. After a quick trip to the bathroom, she put on her clothes from the night before and went in search of Logan. Better to face him now, to see what he was thinking, instead of lying in bed alternately worrying and spinning fantasies that might never come true.

But as she worked her way through the big house, she couldn't find him. Not in any of the bathrooms, not in the family room, not in Luke's room—she'd peeked in and found her son still dead to the world—not on the front porch. As she stood there, taking in the scent and sound of the ocean slowly rolling in, she saw his truck was missing. Logan was gone, without so much as a "Thank you, ma'am."

The hurt that came with the realization was surprisingly sharp, shockingly painful. Even as she told herself it was no big deal, that she'd been anticipating this behavior, she knew she was lying. He'd given her the most beautiful night of her life and part of her—the part that still sighed over fairy tales even though she knew they never happened in real life— had expected him to be here, waiting for her.

She'd hoped to find him in the kitchen, smiling at her over a cup of coffee. Had hoped to find him on the front porch, reading the newspaper and listening to the ocean. Instead he was gone and she was left with a heart that was surprisingly bruised.

She made her way into the kitchen, desperate for some caffeine to dispel the cobwebs still taking up residence in the corners of her mind. If she could get rid of them, she could shake off this stupid melancholy and put aside her disappointment.

She was halfway to the coffeemaker, bag of beans in hand, before the large pink bakery box on the counter registered. Next to it stood two full cups of coffee that were still warm and a stack of napkins with Delilah's scrawled across them.

Paige didn't even try to stop the goofy grin. Logan hadn't snuck out in the middle of the night, desperate to get away from her. He'd stayed until morning, had even driven into town to get breakfast for the three of them. He wasn't here now, but he'd left his coffee behind—almost as if he'd left in a huge hurry. He must have gotten an emergency call from work and run out to deal with it. Such was the life of a small-town sheriff, or so she assumed.

Reaching for the coffee he'd left her, she took a long sip, savoring the warmth as it flowed through her system. But even as she drank, she had a feeling that the heat inside of her had much more to do with her feelings for Logan than it did the coffee.

It was a scary thought given their history. But she wasn't going to think about that today, she told herself firmly. She wasn't going to worry about the future when the present was so glorious.

Taking her coffee and a chocolate croissant out to the porch, she sat on the swing and simply watched the ocean roll in. She didn't want to think anymore, didn't want to second and third and fourth guess Logan's motives. Didn't want to worry about what every word and facial expression meant. That was the stuff of teenagers and she was no longer one. She might have loved Logan since she was seventeen—even as she'd hated him—but that didn't mean that she had to behave like she was still a child. She was a grown woman and smart enough to know that what was meant to happen would happen and there wasn't a lot she could do about it.

Yet she still found herself listening for the phone to ring, or for the sound of Logan's truck in the driveway.

Neither had happened by the time Luke made his

way downstairs an hour and a half later, still a little bleary-eyed from the fun he'd had the night before.

"Hey, Mom."

"Hey, baby. Why don't you come sit over here with me?" She lifted her arm to indicate that he should snuggle against her.

"Did you sleep well?" she asked as he settled in against her.

He yawned, stretched a little. "Yeah. But I wish it was nighttime already."

"You know if you're still tired, you can go back to sleep. It's not like there's anything we have to do today, except more painting."

"I like to paint. But I want it to be night because Dad said he'd take us bowling after his shift, remember? He gets off at six."

She had forgotten and Luke's words erased any lingering concerns she might have had over Logan's disappearance. If he was off at six that night, it probably meant he had to work the first shift, which she'd learned started early. She'd hear from him sometime during the day—he always called to confirm plans with Luke before he picked him up.

But as the day passed and she and Luke painted a third guest room—peach this time—Logan didn't call. When she took Luke outside to throw the football, she brought her cell phone in case, but no call. And when six o'clock came and went with no sign of

Logan and no phone call to cancel, the first stirrings of anger started to well inside of her.

It was one thing to sleep with her then disappear. It had been years since that had happened to her, but it had indeed happened in the past. But to make plans with her son and blow them off—blow *him* off? She wasn't okay with that and when Logan finally did get around to calling, she was going to tell him exactly what she thought of his behavior.

Luke seemed to take being stood up fairly well, considering how much he'd been looking forward to going bowling. But he kept telling her it was no big deal, that his dad probably had some big arrest at work. It had nearly broken her heart when he'd smiled and said, "The son of a police officer has to learn to be flexible. Bad things don't happen on a schedule."

For Luke, she tried to keep the faith. Tried to tell herself the same thing—that Logan was stuck at work and unable to get away. But even as she told herself that, even as she agreed with her son that his father's absence didn't mean anything, deep inside she knew the truth. Logan regretted sleeping with her and was running away. Like most men of her acquaintance, he couldn't handle being honest about it, so he was staying away until she got the hint.

And boy, did she get it. He wouldn't have to worry about her making any unpleasant scenes this time around, begging him to take her back, to believe her, to want her and her child. She'd learned her lesson last time, even if she had had a relapse.

But that relapse was over, her heart was once again hardened against him. When he called, she would tell him so, tell him he could see Luke because he had nothing to fear from her.

That's how stupid she was. How unbelievably moronic she was. That she really believed Logan would eventually call or stop by. That he would want to see his son, whom he'd sworn was the best part of his day.

Two days later, when Penny finally made it back from Portland, Paige and Luke were still waiting for the phone to ring.

"If you're so mad, why don't you call him yourself?" Penny asked, as they sanded an armoire she had picked up in Portland for a song. Four days had passed since Logan had made love to Paige then pulled his disappearing act and she couldn't remember ever feeling so angry or guilty in her life.

If she hadn't slept with him, things would still be fine. He would still be showing up every day to take Luke on some fun outing, still be hanging out on the porch talking easily to her. He would still be the man she'd wanted to believe he was.

Instead, she had done something stupid, something

she'd sworn she would never do again and everything had gone to hell. And what bothered her the most, what hurt her the way nothing else could, was that she wasn't the only one suffering from her mistake. Luke was devastated by his father's desertion, confused and hurt and wondering what he had done wrong.

She told him every day that it wasn't his fault, that he'd had nothing to do with Logan's disappearance, but he didn't believe her. How could he? In his mind, his father had said he'd loved him then changed his mind. The dad he knew wouldn't do that without a reason. He wouldn't do it if Luke hadn't screwed up.

"Why should I call him?" she demanded as she took her anger out on the armoire, sanding for all she was worth. "He's the one who disappeared without a trace."

"Exactly. Which is a pretty good indicator that he's not going to call. If you want to know what happened, you're going to have to be the bigger person."

"I already know exactly what happened. The same thing that always happens with Logan. He got a shiny new toy and wanted to play with it. But after a while that toy got boring and he dropped it like it never existed, like he never really wanted it at all. Typical modus operandi for Logan Powell—I was the idiot who forgot. So I guess this whole mess is really my fault."

Penny sat back on her haunches and Paige

pretended not to notice the way her sister was studying her. It didn't work. "I have to say, sis, that's the first time I have ever heard you refer to yourself as a toy."

Paige shot her a fulminating glare. "It was a metaphor and I was referring to Luke. That kid is in his bedroom right now, trying to figure out what the hell he did wrong to make his father not want to be with him. It's awful. This whole thing is awful."

Penny nodded her agreement. "I still can't believe you slept with him. What were you thinking?"

"I don't know. I wasn't thinking. Obviously."

"Obviously."

"But if you could have seen him that night. He was so tender, so sweet, so different than he'd ever been with me. It was impossible to say no."

"Maybe he felt the same way." Penny held up a hand to stay Paige's vehement denial. "I'm not defending the rat, believe me. Watching my nephew mope around like it's the end of the world has been no fun. But you told me yesterday that things had been so intense between the two of you that it scared you a little. Maybe Logan felt the same way."

"I doubt it. If he'd felt even half of what I did, there's no way he'd be able to stay away. But again, this isn't about me. It's about Luke."

"It's about both of you."

"No, it isn't."

"Yes, it is. Because if it was only about Luke, you would have been beating Logan's door down two days ago, demanding to know who the hell he thought he was to mess with your kid."

"That's not true."

"When have you ever let anyone hurt Luke without taking them on?" When Paige didn't answer, Penny smirked at her. "See? Never. Which means you're as hurt by his behavior as Luke is and you don't want to deal with it."

"Since when are you a psychologist?" Paige tried to ignore the fact that her sister was right. She was hurt by Logan's behavior, and even worse, she felt like a moron.

She'd spent the past nine years growing strong, protecting herself and her child, making sure that no man could ever hurt her again. She'd kept to herself, dating only casually, if at all, in an effort to protect herself. To protect Luke. Not because she believed all men were scum, but because she knew one man was and she wanted to make sure she didn't make a similar mistake.

She laughed bitterly. Well, she had to hand it to herself. She hadn't done what she'd feared—hadn't made a similar mistake. Oh, no. Not her. She'd made the same damn mistake with the same damn man. It was humbling, and horrifying, to realize that despite everything, she really hadn't learned a thing.

So what was she supposed to do? Should she let this go? Ignore Logan and hope that in time Luke would grow to understand that his father's deficiencies had nothing to do with him? Should she talk to her son, admit her mistakes—past and present? Or should she confront Logan, force him to be the father that Luke needed?

She and Luke had been good on their own for a lot of years. No Logan meant no interference, no threat of a custody battle, no having to share Luke. She'd be lying if she didn't admit that that thought appealed to her, especially in light of recent events.

But just because it was the path of least resistance, didn't mean it was necessarily the right one. Luke had wanted a father figure for a long time. His father. That had become glaringly obvious in the days he spent with Logan.

Was it fair to deprive him of that, simply because it was easier for her not to deal with Logan? Penny was right. Paige had always fought for Luke, from the moment he was born. Had always been willing to take on anyone and anything in an effort to make her son's life better.

So why wasn't she doing that now? Why wasn't she confronting Logan and demanding that he take responsibility for his son? Not monetarily—Luke had everything he needed and then some—but emotionally. Why wasn't she taking him on, when it was obvious that her son needed him? Wanted him?

The answer, when it came to her, wasn't pleasant, but it galvanized her. She had let Logan do this again—to her and her son—because she was a coward. She was afraid of what he could do to her, of how he could make her feel, and she was hiding out at Penny's because it meant she didn't have to deal with him. Didn't have to face her own weaknesses and failures when it came to Logan Powell.

But no more. She was done with that, just as she was done with him. But he had responsibilities to Luke. He was the one who had opened this can of worms, the one who had insisted he wanted to be a part of Luke's life. Now it was time for him to ante up.

This was it. She'd give him one more chance and if he didn't come through for Luke now, then he was done. She didn't care how loud he yelled or how many scenes he caused or how many lawyers he got, there would be no way she was letting him within one hundred yards of her child.

## CHAPTER SEVENTEEN

LOGAN LET HIMSELF INTO the house through the garage. After grabbing a beer, he flopped down on the sofa and turned on the TV. It wasn't until he'd twisted off the cap that it occurred to him that he was doing that a lot lately—coming home and getting buzzed in an effort to avoid thinking.

About Luke. About Paige. About the gigantic mess he had managed to make of all of their lives.

He put down the beer with a frown of disgust. The last thing he wanted was to turn into his mother—dealing with the difficult parts of life through a substance-induced haze. Oh, his mother's haze came from her prescription tranquilizers, but denial was denial was denial.

He'd started to call Paige at least fifty times over the past few days, wanting to explain. Wanting to apologize for running out on both her and Luke. But every time he dialed her number, he heard his mother's devastated voice in his head and he'd hung up, too afraid of ending up bitter, miserable, trapped to actually dial the phone.

He knew he was going to have to eventually. After all, he needed to see Luke. The days had passed with agonizing slowness and he knew that part of the reason was because he missed his son. It was amazing how fast he'd grown used to seeing the kid every day, how knowing he had an outing planned made the day go faster.

But he wasn't ready to face Paige yet, not even if it was to talk about their son. He needed a little more time to gird his defenses, to bury the hurt and the guilt and the sorrow so that they didn't spill over her the second he opened his mouth.

Reaching for the remote control, he flipped channels until he found a baseball game. Washington was playing Boston tonight. It promised to be a good game—he needed something to take his mind off his problems.

But he'd barely watched an inning when his doorbell rang. Cursing under his breath, he went to answer it, prepared to tell whoever was on the other side to leave him the hell alone.

He nearly fell over at the sight of Paige on his porch. Paige had come to see him.

But she didn't look like any Paige he had ever seen before. Dressed in an expensive black pantsuit with an emerald silk blouse and black stiletto heels, she looked every inch the successful businesswoman she was. She also looked completely untouchable and about as inviting.

"Can I come in?" she asked.

"Sure, yeah, of course." He stopped gaping like an idiot and stepped aside so she could come in. "Can I get you a drink?"

"No, thank you. I wouldn't exactly call this a social call."

Something about her attitude pricked at him. Maybe it was the stiff way she held herself away from him or the look in her eye that said he was about three levels below the ugliest, most pathetic bug she could imagine. Whatever it was, he found himself wanting to get to her. Wanting to muss up her perfect look a little bit, until he could find the Paige he knew—the real Paige—wherever she'd hidden her.

Unable to resist, he shoved his hands in his pockets and leaned indolently against the wall. "Okay, darlin'. I'll bite. If this isn't a social call, what exactly is it?" He let his eyes sweep over her from head to toe, lingering on her full mouth, beautiful breasts and long, long legs.

Her eyes narrowed and he felt his body react to her challenge, felt himself grow hard when arousal was the last thing he should be feeling. Hadn't he promised himself that he was done with her, that he wouldn't do this? His sanity couldn't take it.

And yet, being in the same room with her made

him want to forget every vow he'd made. She was so damn sexy and smart, so damn perfect for him, that keeping his hands off of her was agony.

"Look, Logan, I don't care about what happened between us. I don't care that you snuck out of my house or that you didn't call me or that things didn't work out."

"You don't care?" he asked, moving toward her slowly. Crowding her so that she retreated across the room.

"No."

"Not at all?"

"Absolutely not." But her voice didn't sound as certain as it had moments ago. Which was exactly what he'd been looking for. Because he cared that things weren't working out between them. He cared so much it was ripping him apart and he needed her to feel some of the confusion and need and desperation that was roiling inside him.

He stroked his hand down her satiny cheek, brushed his thumb over her sweet, pink lips. They parted on a gasp and her eyes turned cloudy in an instant.

"Are you sure?" he asked, leaning toward her, until his mouth was only centimeters from her ear. Though she didn't give an inch, a shudder worked its way through her and he grinned. "Because from where I'm standing, it looks like you care a whole hell of a lot."

"You really are a bastard, you know that?" Her voice trembled and he told himself to stop. Told himself that he was, indeed, being a bastard. Whatever he started here wasn't going to end well—that much was obvious. And yet he couldn't help himself. He needed to touch her, needed to feel her body against his one more time.

"If I'm such a bastard, why aren't you moving away?" He brought his other hand up, cupped her breast. Toyed with her diamond-hard nipple. "Why are you letting me touch you? Why are you all but shaking with desire?"

He lowered his mouth, brushed his lips against hers as he waited for her to react. This time, he wanted her to be the one to take him. Her to make the final move that brought their mouths into brutal, brilliant contact.

He was on fire, his body aching for her. His heart crying out for her even as he told himself it was useless. That loving her was hurtful, abhorrent, wrong. That she would hurt him again and again before things were finally over between them.

But none of his arguments mattered, none of the promises he'd made to himself were worth a damn. Because the second he'd opened that door he'd known that nothing mattered but Paige and his son. And nothing ever would.

She didn't make the final move, didn't bring her mouth to his, so in the end he did it for her. He curled his hand around the back of her head and brought her forward, until her lips touched his.

Lust exploded in him the second their mouths met, and he went at her like a starving man. Thrusting his tongue between her lips, he explored every part of her honeyed depths before stroking along her tongue with his own.

He kissed her until he felt as though he was going to implode, taking everything she had to give and demanding more. More. More. Paige whimpered against him, her hands going to his shoulders and still he didn't relinquish her. He couldn't. He needed this, needed her, in a way he'd never needed anything or anyone in his entire life. And no matter how much she was going to hurt him in the end, there was no way he could let her go.

Except he had to, because suddenly she was shoving at him, her hands pushing against his chest as she struggled to get out of his embrace.

He let go the instant it registered that she wanted him to stop, stepped back and simply looked at her as he ran his tongue over his lips in an effort to pull more of her inside himself. But then he looked at her, really looked at her. The trembling he'd thought was from passion was actually from grief. Her eyes burned with tears.

"Paige." He reached for her with the intent of comforting her, but she pulled away so hard that she stumbled.

"Don't touch me. Don't you dare touch me ever again."

Her words slammed through him with the power of a semi. "I don't understand. I can feel how much you want me."

"I want a lot of things, Logan, but not all of them are good for me. *You're* not good for me."

Her words so closely echoed his thoughts that he would have laughed if he didn't feel like he was being ripped apart. "You're unbelievable, you know that?"

"I'm unbelievable? You're the one who slept with me, dumped me, dumped your kid."

"That's ancient history. I'm not the same man."

"Aren't you?" She arched an eyebrow. "Because I wasn't talking about nine years ago. I was talking about now."

"I didn't dump you."

"What would you call it?"

"I was confused. I needed some time to think—"

"Oh, really? *You* needed time?"

"Yes, damn it. I won't apologize for that. I had to come to grips with what I feel for you. When you cheated on me nine years ago, it nearly killed me. I know we were young, know that it wasn't supposed to matter. But I loved you then, loved you with everything I had. Knowing that you didn't feel the same way made me crazy.

"I didn't want to be like that again. Didn't want to lose myself to you so completely that you could hurt me like that again."

Paige laughed, but it was a harsh, bitter sound that set everything inside him on red alert. "I hurt you? *I* hurt *you?* You've got some nerve, you know that?"

"Paige, don't do this. I want—"

"Do you think I give a damn what you want at this point? You're sitting over here, nursing imagined wounds from nearly a decade ago while I'm at home trying to figure out how to explain to my eight-year-old son why his daddy doesn't want to talk to him anymore. Why he didn't show up to take him bowling like he'd promised. Why he hasn't so much as called him in five days."

Remorse filled him at her words, nearly brought him to his knees. "I'm sorry. I'll make it up to him. I needed to—"

She shook her head and the look in her eyes was filled with a contempt he'd never imagined seeing from her. "*You want. You need.* Isn't that the problem? Hasn't that always been the problem? In your head, it's all Logan, all the time, and to hell with what anyone else wants or needs. Well, I'm done with it and I'm done with you. Don't come near me or my son, ever again."

She turned on her five-inch heels and headed for the door at such a fast walk it was almost a run.

"Paige, wait!"

"I've waited long enough, Logan. I'm done waiting and so is your son."

He slammed his palm against the door seconds before she got to it. "You can't do this. You can't keep my son from me."

"As if I'd have to. You're doing an excellent job of that all by yourself."

She reached for the door handle, tried to pull it open, but he wouldn't let go. He couldn't. Panic had set in and all he could think about was keeping her there until he could convince her that she was wrong about him. That he wasn't a selfish, self-absorbed bastard. That he did care about someone other than himself.

"Let go of the door, Logan."

"Not yet." He willed her to turn around, willed her to look at him, but she didn't so much as move.

"Paige." He laid a soft hand on her back, was shocked to realize that she was trembling despite the hardass act she was putting on. It made him feel terrible even as it gave him hope. "Paige, please."

At first he thought she wasn't going to answer, but finally she said, "What?"

"I never meant to hurt you. I swear."

She did look at him then, her beautiful features contorted into a sneer. "As if you could."

She grabbed the door handle, yanked as hard as she could. And because he was still reeling from her words—from the look of utter hatred she had leveled at him—he let his hand fall away.

Then she walked down his steps, leaving him with the knowledge that he had let the only thing that had ever truly mattered to him slip right through his fingers.

## CHAPTER EIGHTEEN

PAIGE FINISHED PLANTING the last group of flowers in the front yard, then stepped back to admire her handiwork. There were bright pinks and yellows and reds—cheerful colors that looked incredibly happy against the newly painted picket fence that rimmed the yard. Luke had chosen the plants in town the other day, and she had fallen in love with them the second he'd pointed them out.

Stretching, she rested her hands on her lower back, which still ached from the marathon painting session she and Penny had embarked on the day before. Then she turned and stared at the ocean beyond the cliffs that bordered her sister's land to the west. Three weeks had passed since her last fight with Logan, five weeks since she and Luke had arrived here, and a lot had changed.

Penny's beach house was almost finished. With the added influx of capital from Paige, she'd managed to get the plumbing and electric fixed in record time. And they had finished nearly all the rooms—painting, stripping the hardwood, staining it, arranging the furniture and hanging curtains. If things stayed on track, Penny might be able to open by the end of July. It was a little late in the season, but they both figured catching half the summer was better than missing it completely, as they'd originally planned on.

And it wasn't as if there weren't tourists around looking for places to stay. In the past couple of weeks, the beach in front of the inn had filled up as flocks of tourists had moved in, laughing and surfing and building sandcastles on the stretch of beach Paige had somehow started to consider hers. They annoyed her, with their happy chatter and carefree games.

And yet she watched them religiously, took Luke down to the sand to play with the children nearly every day. And wondered what it would be like to be part of a family like that. With a mom and a dad and children, all of whom were secure in the love of the other members of the family. All of whom knew exactly where they belonged.

She was getting maudlin, a surefire sign that she'd had too much time to think. Better to go upstairs and get started retiling the last bathroom. Penny and Luke had gone to town to get more grout, but there was enough left that she could get started. If she kept busy, she wouldn't be able to brood about Logan and the absolute mess he had made of her and Luke's lives.

She was halfway up the stairs between the second and third floors when the phone rang. She almost left it to the answering machine, but some sixth sense she was barely aware of told her to answer it. Taking the stairs two at a time, she managed to reach it as the answering machine clicked on.

"Hello."

"Paige, it's Logan."

She hated that her heart beat faster at the sound of his voice, hated more that tears welled behind her eyelids. This whole thing stunk. She wanted to escape to L.A., where she wouldn't have to hear about him or think about him whenever she had a few moments of down time.

But then, when she thought of never running into him again—never seeing him again—something deep inside her screamed in protest. It was an untenable situation, one that was slowly driving her out of her mind.

Forcing herself to be strong, she injected steel into her voice in an effort to keep him from finding out how much he affected her. "I can't talk right now, Logan. I'm in the middle—"

"There's been an accident. Luke and Penny are at the hospital. It's pretty bad—"

The phone slipped from her hand, hit the floor as Logan's words replayed in her head. Then she was running for the front door, grabbing her purse on the way.

The drive to the hospital usually took close to thirty minutes—it was halfway between Prospect and Sunshine, another small Oregon coastal town. She did it in fifteen minutes, praying the entire way.

Panic was alive within her, making it nearly impossible for her to think as she drove into the first parking spot she saw then ran for the emergency room doors. She didn't know what was wrong, didn't know who to talk to, didn't know anything—

Luke, oh, God, Luke. Penny. A sob welled in her chest. Later. There would be time enough to cry later after she knew how bad they were. After she'd seen her sister and her baby.

The first thing she saw in the emergency room was Logan, standing to the right of the doors, his silver eyes fastened on the entrance.

Suddenly his strong arms were around her, holding her up when her knees would have buckled. "Tell me," she said against his chest. "Luke. Penny. Please. Tell me about my baby."

"There isn't much to tell. They were involved in a head-on collision with a bunch of drunk teenagers who were driving on the wrong side of the road. Luke was unconscious when we got to the scene and he hasn't woken up yet. They're doing some tests now, a CAT scan and a few other things trying to see if—" His voice broke. "Trying to see if there's any damage."

"Damage?" she asked, trying to comprehend what he was saying…and what he wasn't.

"Brain damage, Paige. He hit his head really hard and they're trying to see—"

Not even Logan's strong hands could keep her from sliding to the floor. "He might be…"

"They don't know." He crouched down next to her.

"Well, what do they know?" she shrieked.

"Nothing yet. It's going to be a while."

"Oh, my God. Oh, my God. Where's the doctor? And why aren't you with Luke?"

"I was with him, Paige. They took him away to run the tests and the nurse promised to come get me as soon as he was back in the ER."

"I want to see him. I need to see him, Logan."

"You will, baby. I promise. As soon as he gets back, I'll take you to him."

She nodded, but she could barely understand the words coming out of his mouth, could barely comprehend where she was and what she was doing there. Logan lifted a hand to her face, brushed her hair back from her eyes. As he did, she realized he was trembling. Big, tough Logan Powell was shaking like a leaf.

She wrapped her hand around his and held it to

her chest, trying to comfort him as he was her. "And Penny? What about my sister?"

"She's going to be fine. She has a number of cuts, a few deep lacerations to her arms. She's getting stitches right now, but the doctor said she'd be able to go home today."

"Thank God."

"Do you want to see her? She was upset about Luke so they had to sedate her. I think she could really use a hug from you right about now."

"Yeah, of course." She looked around the emergency room blindly. She knew she needed to get up but she couldn't seem to move, to think, to function.

Logan stood, then slowly eased her to her feet. "I've got you."

"I can't do—"

"You don't have to do anything. Let me take care of you." He wrapped his arm around her waist and guided her carefully toward the admittance desk.

The nurse must have recognized him because she buzzed them through and then she was standing outside the room where a doctor stitched a long gash on Penny's shoulder.

Paige started to shake as she looked at her sister, shocked at how much blood there was on her. Her shirt had been cut off and lay discarded on the floor. It was drenched in blood, as were her jeans and much of her skin. To Paige's shame, all she could think about was if her sister looked this bad and was deemed all right, what did her child look like?

The doctor finished with the cut and as he prepared to do the next one, Logan pushed open the door, nudging her inside as he did so. Both Penny and the doctor looked up as they entered, and though it seemed like the doctor was going to object to their presence, an intimidating look from Logan had him snapping his mouth shut.

"I'm so sorry! Oh, God, Paige, I'm so sorry. I tried to get him out. I tried—"

"Shh, Penny. Stop." She crossed the room in two strides, and ran a soothing hand down her sister's hair. She wanted to hug her, but Penny was so banged up she couldn't figure out how to do it without hurting her. "It's not your fault."

"It is my fault. It is. I saw them, but I couldn't stop. I couldn't get out of the way—"

"I just got her calmed down enough to work on her," the doctor said. "If you're going to upset her again, you'll have to leave."

Paige ignored him. Grabbing her sister's hands, she said, "Penny, stop it. Just stop it. Logan was there, at the site. You did everything you could. This isn't your fault."

"But—"

"It isn't your fault, Penny," Logan said. "You have

to calm down and let the doctor take care of you, or he's going to knock you out and you'll be stuck here until tomorrow. We're here, they're taking care of Luke. Everything that can be done is being done."

Paige didn't know if it was his words or the authoritative way he delivered them, but Penny lay against the hospital bed with a shuddering breath. Tears leaked from her eyes and Paige's heart broke for her sister.

"I need to finish stitching her," the doctor said, though his voice had warmed considerably from when they'd first entered the room.

"Can she stay?" Penny whispered, her hand clutching at Paige's.

"I'm not going anywhere, Penny. So you squeeze my hand until your heart's content."

HOURS LATER, LOGAN STOOD BY Luke's bedside with Paige and waited for the doctor to come discuss the results of all the tests they'd been running on him since he'd been admitted. Luke had been moved to pediatric ICU, something Logan didn't interpret as a good sign, and he was going crazy with the unknown.

A quick glance at Paige showed that she was as pale as he felt. She had Luke's hand clutched in her own, and she was whispering soothing words to him, though he had yet to regain consciousness. Her eyes were red, her jaw tight, but she was holding it together better than he was. Who would have guessed?

He glanced at the clock, saw that only three minutes had passed since the last time he looked. They'd been the three longest minutes of his life, this afternoon the longest afternoon of his life, and if a doctor didn't get in here and talk to them soon, he wasn't going to be responsible for his actions. Officer of the law, be damned. He would beat the information out of the staff if he had to.

"He's going to be fine," Paige whispered.

"Of course he is."

"No. You need to say it like you believe it, Logan. Luke is going to be fine. He's going to walk away from this. He's going to—" Her voice broke, but she didn't cry. Didn't so much as tear up.

"Paige."

He reached for her free hand, held it in his own. And though he had meant to comfort her, in the end, he was the one who was comforted. So much so that the excruciatingly slow passage of time somehow become a little more bearable.

It was nearly nine o'clock before a doctor came in. He was young and tired looking and Logan instantly distrusted him—a feeling that only grew when the doctor called him Mr. Matthews.

"How's my son?" he demanded, barely conscious

of the fact that Paige's fingernails were digging into the back of his hand.

"To be honest, we're not sure yet." The doctor walked over to the computer on the table against the wall and pulled up some images of Luke's brain. "If you look here, you can see that there is some swelling in his brain, particularly around the frontal lobe." The doctor traced the image with his pen.

"There's also a shadow over here that concerns us." Again, he used the pen as a pointer. "It's in the premotor cortex, which affects voluntary movement of the body."

"He's paralyzed?" Logan asked, as the world around him turned gray.

"First of all, it's way too early to even consider that. I don't think paralysis is going to be a problem, based on the area of the brain I'm seeing injury in. But swelling does hide a lot, so we'll do another CAT scan tomorrow morning, and a third probably tomorrow evening. Just to see where we stand."

"Where do we stand right now, Dr. Roberts?" Paige spoke for the first time. "I won't hold you to anything you say right now, but please, tell me what you think. What's going on with Luke?"

"He started to come around earlier, but due to the swelling we're keeping him unconscious. If it goes down as I expect it to, we should be able to bring him around tomorrow evening or the following morning.

As for damage, symptoms…" He shook his head. "I just don't know yet. This part of the brain isn't responsible for the ability to move different body parts, simply the ability to coordinate movements. Walking, for example, requires the motion of both legs, the swinging of the arms, et cetera. Hitting a baseball requires the arms, legs, hands, back, shoulders. Damage to this area normally results in some jerkiness of movement, or lack of coordination. An inability to smoothly coordinate all of these body parts together.

"But nothing is guaranteed right now. And everything depends on how or if the swelling goes down on its own. I know that's not what you want to hear, but this is a waiting game. We have to watch for a little while and see what happens. See how much Luke's body can heal itself. Once that happens, we'll have a better idea."

Vaguely, Logan was aware he had started to sway. Paige wrapped an arm around his waist to bolster him as she continued asking questions of the doctor that Logan hadn't even thought about. Questions that he knew would have occurred to him two minutes after the doctor walked out of the room.

As the doctor wound down, Logan felt his stomach twist. He couldn't do this, couldn't sit in this tiny little room with his son—*his son*—and wait to find out what was going to happen. Wait to find out if Luke was going to be okay. Wait to see—

A sob rose in his throat. But he couldn't cry. Not here and not now. Not when Paige managed to hold herself together so well.

After the doctor left, she sank into the chair by Luke's bed, stroked a gentle hand over their son's forehead again and again. Her hand was trembling, yet she somehow managed to keep it together. Not one tear leaked down her cheek, not one complaint or lamentation crossed her lips.

She talked softly to Luke, telling him how much she loved him. How much they all did. And how much she was looking forward to looking into his eyes again.

As he watched her, Logan began to understand how a scared seventeen-year-old with almost no options had managed to not only survive but flourish in a city that was known for crushing people into dust. How she had managed to care for a baby by herself, while working full time and getting a degree. How she had managed to achieve so much more than most people who had never had to fight half as hard.

There was no back-up in her, no give, no weakness. No matter what life threw at her, she met it head on. And if, God forbid, something ended up being seriously wrong with Luke, he knew she would deal with that, too. She knew no other way.

It took his breath away. *She* took his breath away.

As he reached out and squeezed Luke's knee, Paige's gaze met his. She looked exhausted, but he knew she would last as long as she had to. She would stay by their son's side as long as he needed her.

And that's when it hit him, what an incredible fool he had been three weeks ago—and nine years ago. A woman like this, so steadfast, so sure of herself, so convinced of right and wrong, would never do what he had accused her of. She would never cheat on him, any more than she would toss him out on his own and leave him to sink or swim.

The realization shattered him, nearly brought him to his knees right there in the middle of the hospital room. Only Paige's strength kept him upright.

But he couldn't take it, couldn't stand being in a room with her and drawing comfort from her when he had wronged her so completely. Mumbling a semi-coherent excuse, he stumbled out and down the hall to the elevator. He was desperate to get outside so he could breathe.

But when he was in the parking lot, taking huge lungfuls of air into his shuddering chest, he still couldn't steady himself. He was breaking apart, into a million pieces. All the ways he'd wronged Paige and his son were unfolding before him and he couldn't stand it. Couldn't stand what he'd done to them. Couldn't stand that he might never get a chance to make it right with Luke.

*Dear God, please, not Luke.* Not his son. Not Paige's son. *Please God, don't take him from Paige. She couldn't—*

Logan's legs collapsed beneath him and he hit the ground hard. He knew he had to get up, knew he had to go inside to sit with Luke and Paige. He'd failed in so many ways already, he couldn't fail them again. Not now. Not in this.

Yet he couldn't make his legs move. Couldn't find the will to pick himself up. *Dear God, please not Luke. Please, not Luke. Give him another chance. Please God, give me one more chance.* He wouldn't squander it this time. This time he would do everything right. *Please…*

## CHAPTER NINETEEN

WHEN PENNY CAME INTO Luke's room a few minutes later, Paige asked her sister to stay with him while she went looking for Logan. She didn't know where he'd disappeared to, but he'd looked awful when he'd stumbled out and the last thing she needed was for him to be wandering around the hospital in shock.

She asked about him at the nurse's station, and was told that he'd taken one of the elevators. A part of her shriveled up, convinced that Logan had cut and run as he was famous for doing when things got too tough. But she looked for him anyway. She couldn't help it. She kept hearing his voice tell her that he would take care of her this time around.

After checking the waiting rooms on each floor, the entire ER and half the ground floor of the hospital, she'd about given up on him. But that sixth sense told her to keep looking. Stepping out into the parking lot, she scanned the area, not really expecting him to be out there.

She spotted him, sitting on the ground near the empty ambulance bay. His arms were wrapped around his middle as if he was trying to keep himself from flying apart and as she got closer, she realized there were tears pouring down his face.

She started running then, didn't stop until she was kneeling on the ground beside him. "Logan," she said, taking his hands in hers. "It's going to be okay. I swear it. Come on, sweetheart. Please, don't do this to yourself."

"I'm fine." He looked away, wiped his face, tried his best to hide his tears from her.

"You are not fine. Talk to me, Logan."

He reached out then, dragging her into his arms and burying his face in the curve where her shoulder met her neck. Her arms went around him automatically and even as she told herself it was a bad idea to let him in again, Paige couldn't stop herself from melting against him. It felt so good to be held by him, so right.

"I'm sorry." His voice was barely audible.

"What?"

"I'm sorry. I was stupid, an ass, completely blind. I hurt you again and again when you've never done anything but love me."

Paige looked at him, shocked, but he clutched at her, trying desperately to keep her body pressed against his.

"I'm sorry. So sorry. I don't deserve you and Luke, not after everything I've done, but I love you. And I swear to you that I won't ever turn my back on you again. I won't ever leave you alone again. I swear it, Paige. I swear it."

"Hush, Logan." She smoothed his hair back from his face. "This isn't the time to worry about that—"

"It's exactly the time. I almost lost him today. I've already lost you and I can't stand it. I can't stand knowing that I hurt you, that I left you alone, that I didn't protect the two of you the way I should have."

She was crying now, too, silent tears as she rested her forehead against his.

"Please don't cry, Paige. Please, darlin'. I never meant to make you cry. You were mine. It was my job to make sure you were okay and instead, I hurt you worse than anybody. I'm sorry. I'm so sorry. Give me another chance and I promise I'll never screw up again."

She ran a hand down his cheek. And as she looked into his beautiful, beloved face, she realized that she couldn't keep hiding behind the past. She'd spent nine years running away from her emotions, and the past six weeks running away from Logan. Frightened of being hurt again. Frightened of opening herself up.

But here they were anyway, scared, aching, desperate. Worried about their son might have to go through and the pain they'd already caused each other. It was stupid, ridiculous, to hold on to the past.

The Logan in front of her was not the Logan from nine years ago, and she was not that girl, either. They had both grown and matured, had both survived. And they were both still here. That was going to have to be enough for her, because life didn't come with any better guarantees.

"Of course you'll screw up again," she told him, laughing. "And so will I. And then we'll forgive each other, because that's what people who love each other do."

"You love me?"

"I've always loved you. Even when we wanted to kill each other, I loved you. It's why there's never been another man for me, not from the moment you first looked at me. It's why there will never be another man for me."

"I'm sorry—"

"Shh." She placed her fingers over his lips. "No more apologies. From either of us. The past is dead, over. It's just us now. The three of us, moving forward from here. Okay?"

He nodded. "More than okay."

"Good." She brushed her lips across his once, twice, took him deep inside herself, where she promised herself never to let him go again. Then she climbed slowly to her feet, held a hand out to him.

"Let's go to our son and get started on that future you promised me."

Logan took her hand and they walked toward the hospital, together.

## EPILOGUE

Two weeks later, Logan carried Luke through the front door of his house. "Jeez, I can walk, Dad."

"Humor the old man, kid. It's been a long couple of weeks."

And it had. The first few days after the accident had been a nightmare the likes of which Logan had never experienced. The second and third CAT scans had undefined results—there remained so much swelling around Luke's brain that it had been impossible to tell how severe the damage might be.

They'd been told to wait and pray for their son to open his eyes. He'd finally done it, four days after the accident, and Logan had never been happier than when Luke had reached out a hand for him and called him Daddy.

They'd done another CAT scan later that day, followed by an MRI and a number of other tests. The results were the same. As the doctor had originally suspected, there was a small amount of damage to the part of the brain that controlled gross motor skills on the left side. They believed it could be almost completely corrected over time with physical therapy, but Luke's dreams of being a pro basketball player were probably finished.

Which was okay, he'd told his parents with a grin that was all charm. He'd already decided he wanted to be a doctor, since they got to work with so many pretty nurses all day long.

"I can't believe we're going to be living at your house. This place is so cool!"

"It is, isn't it?" Paige agreed with a smile. "You're not going to miss L.A., are you?"

"No way! I didn't want to tell you when we were living there, but all that smog really bummed me out. And since you can still work on movies from here, I think everything's perfect."

Logan lowered his son to the couch, then sat next to him, pulling Paige into his lap as he did so. She came willingly, snuggling right under his arm and he was so overwhelmed with emotions, that for a moment he couldn't do anything but breathe. He didn't know what he'd ever done in his life to deserve these two people, but he did know thing. He was never letting go of them again.

* * * * *

# COMING NEXT MONTH

### Available May 10, 2011

You can find more information on upcoming
Harlequin® titles, free excerpts and more at
**www.HarlequinInsideRomance.com.**

HSRCNM0411

# REQUEST YOUR FREE BOOKS!
## 2 FREE NOVELS PLUS 2 FREE GIFTS!

### Harlequin *Super Romance*

### Exciting, emotional, unexpected!

**YES!** Please send me 2 FREE Harlequin® Superromance® novels and my 2 FREE gifts (gifts are worth about $10). After receiving them, if I don't wish to receive any more books, I can return the shipping statement marked "cancel." If I don't cancel, I will receive 6 brand-new novels every month and be billed just $4.69 per book in the U.S. or $5.24 per book in Canada. That's a saving of at least 15% off the cover price! It's quite a bargain! Shipping and handling is just 50¢ per book in the U.S. and 75¢ per book in Canada.* I understand that accepting the 2 free books and gifts places me under no obligation to buy anything. I can always return a shipment and cancel at any time. Even if I never buy another book, the two free books and gifts are mine to keep forever.

135/336 HDN FC6T

| Name | (PLEASE PRINT) | |
|------|------|------|
| Address | | Apt. # |
| City | State/Prov. | Zip/Postal Code |

Signature (if under 18, a parent or guardian must sign)

### Mail to the **Reader Service:**
**IN U.S.A.:** P.O. Box 1867, Buffalo, NY 14240-1867
**IN CANADA:** P.O. Box 609, Fort Erie, Ontario L2A 5X3

**Not valid for current subscribers to Harlequin Superromance books.**
**Are you a current subscriber to Harlequin Superromance books**
**and want to receive the larger-print edition?**
**Call 1-800-873-8635 or visit www.ReaderService.com.**

* Terms and prices subject to change without notice. Prices do not include applicable taxes. Sales tax applicable in N.Y. Canadian residents will be charged applicable taxes. Offer not valid in Quebec. This offer is limited to one order per household. All orders subject to credit approval. Credit or debit balances in a customer's account(s) may be offset by any other outstanding balance owed by or to the customer. Please allow 4 to 6 weeks for delivery. Offer available while quantities last.

**Your Privacy**—The Reader Service is committed to protecting your privacy. Our Privacy Policy is available online at www.ReaderService.com or upon request from the Reader Service.

We make a portion of our mailing list available to reputable third parties that offer products we believe may interest you. If you prefer that we not exchange your name with third parties, or if you wish to clarify or modify your communication preferences, please visit us at www.ReaderService.com/consumerschoice or write to us at Reader Service Preference Service, P.O. Box 9062, Buffalo, NY 14269. Include your complete name and address.

HSR11

*With an evil force hell-bent on destruction,
two enemies must unite to find a truth that turns
all-too-personal when passions collide.*

*Enjoy a sneak peek in Jenna Kernan's next installment
in her original* TRACKER *series,* GHOST STALKER,
*available in May, only from Harlequin Nocturne.*

"**W**ho are you?" he snarled.

Jessie lifted her chin. "Your better."

His smile was cold. "Such arrogance could only come from a Niyanoka."

She nodded. "Why are you here?"

"I don't know." He glanced about her room. "I asked the birds to take me to a healer."

"And they have done so. Is that *all* you asked?"

"No. To lead them away from my friends." His eyes fluttered and she saw them roll over white.

Jessie straightened, preparing to flee, but he roused himself and mastered the momentary weakness. His eyes snapped open, locking on her.

Her heart hammered as she inched back.

"Lead who away?" she whispered, suddenly afraid of the answer.

"The ghosts. Nagi sent them to attack me so I would bring them to her."

The wolf must be deranged because Nagi did not send ghosts to attack living creatures. He captured the evil ones after their death if they refused to walk the Way of Souls, forcing them to face judgment.

"Her? The healer you seek is also female?"

"Michaela. She's Niyanoka, like you. The last Seer of Souls and Nagi wants her dead."

Jessie fell back to her seat on the carpet as the possibility of this ricocheted in her brain. Could it be true?

"Why should I believe you?" But she knew why. His black aura, the part that said he had been touched by death. Only a ghost could do that. But it made no sense.

Why would Nagi hunt one of her people and why would a Skinwalker want to protect her? She had been trained from birth to hate the Skinwalkers, to consider them a threat.

His intent blue eyes pinned her. Jessie felt her mouth go dry as she considered the impossible. Could the trickster be speaking the truth? Great Mystery, what evil was this?

She stared in astonishment. There was only one way to find her answers. But she had never even met a Skinwalker before and so did not even know if they dreamed.

But if he dreamed, she would have her chance to learn the truth.

*Look for GHOST STALKER by Jenna Kernan,*
*available May only from Harlequin Nocturne,*
*wherever books and ebooks are sold.*

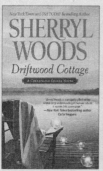
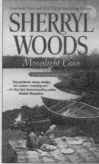